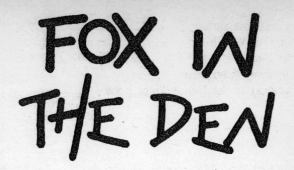

FOX IN THE DEN

Geraldine Witcher

GW01071913

Scripture Union
130 City Road, London EC1V 2NJ.

By the same author:
The Owl Watch
The Picnic
Stowaway Adventure
Runaway in the Den – Tiger Book

© Geraldine Witcher 1991

First Published 1991

ISBN 0 86201 720 3

Phototypeset by Intype, London
Printed and bound in Great Britain by Cox and Wyman Ltd, Reading.

Contents

1

Kit comes home

'Kate! Kate! Kit's coming home today!' Sarah rushed across the wet playground, jumping the puddles as she went, towards her best friend, Kate, sitting sedately on the bench by the door with a brightly coloured umbrella held up over her dark hair.

Kate smiled. 'That's good!' she said. 'It seems ages since we saw him at half term. How long is he staying this time?'

'Until Easter Saturday. His parents are coming over from the Middle East to get him, then they're taking him away somewhere for a couple of weeks at the end of the holidays. He'll be with us for just over a week.'

Kate knew she ought to feel as excited as Sarah. Not only were there only two days of term left before the Easter holidays, but their friend Kit was coming to stay with Sarah, and her older brother Daniel. But Kate had a dreadful headache, and her eyes hurt and she just couldn't feel excited about anything. Still, it was nice that Sarah was happy that Kit was coming.

Kate and her sister Jenny had found Kit last summer – Christopher really, but Kit to his friends – hiding in the church where their father was the vicar. The gang had hidden him in the den at the end of Sarah and Daniel's garden.* Kit had run away from home because he didn't want to go to boarding school, when his parents

*This story is told in 'Runaway in the Den'.

went abroad, but now he'd been at the school for two terms. Although he had been really miserable and homesick for the first term, since he'd gone back after Christmas, he seemed to be enjoying it more, judging from his letters and phone calls. At half terms and whenever the holidays were too short for it to be worth him flying out to meet his parents, it had been arranged that Kit could come to stay with Daniel and Sarah. They hadn't seen him since half term, at the middle of February, and now it was early April.

Just then the bell for morning school went. Sarah jumped up.

'Come on, Kate. I want today to go really quickly. I tried to persuade Dad to let me have the day off and go with him to meet Kit, but he wouldn't.'

'I'm not surprised!' Kate replied, getting up from the bench rather more slowly than her friend. 'My parents never let me have time off school unless I'm really ill. Mum wouldn't even let me stay home today when I didn't feel well earlier. She said to stick it out till the end of term, and that I'm just tired.'

'Are you? You might be getting chicken-pox.'

Kate shuddered. 'I hope not. Not this near the holidays.'

By now the two girls had gone into the cloakroom and hung up their wet coats. Kate took off her wellies and put on her pumps. The classroom was warm and cosy, a bright contrast to the grey stormy day outside. They both found it very difficult to concentrate on school work; Kate, because she didn't feel very well, and Sarah, because she kept thinking about Kit.

'Sarah!' Kate whispered, during maths, 'I'm ever so hot. Are you?'

'It *is* hot in here,' Sarah whispered back.

'I *can't* be getting chicken-pox. If I get it now, I'll miss the church holiday.'

'Mum hasn't let me see Daniel while he's been ill, so I wouldn't catch it,' Sarah told her. 'It's been boring without him.'

'Well, you'll have Kit tonight,' Kate reminded her.

'Great!' said Sarah as she stood up to take her work to be marked.

A bad chicken-pox epidemic had hit the school during the last part of the term. Nearly half the children were away. Daniel, Sarah's brother, had it very badly, and Jenny, Kate's older sister, had gone down with it last week. Robert Bland from the village shop, another member of the Den gang, had been one of the first to get it. Although recovered, he had not come back to school. His mother, who tended to fuss, had sent him to stay with his granny until he was really fit again. Of their gang, this only left at school Sarah and Kate, who hadn't caught it, and James, who had had it when he was small.

A little while later, Kate whispered to Sarah again, 'I do feel funny. I'm hot and itchy, and the numbers on my page won't keep still.' Sarah looked at her friend. Kate was flushed and wriggling in her seat.

'I think you *have* got it!' Sarah whispered back. She put her hand up. 'Miss Turner I think, Kate's got chicken-pox.'

Immediately their teacher had Kate out of the classroom and along to the secretary, and in a very short while Kate too was at home tucked up in bed with strict instructions not to scratch!

The rest of the day dragged even more for Sarah without Kate to talk to, but at last the bell went. Sarah grabbed her coat, and rushed out; and there standing by the gate, grinning, was Kit! It took less than two seconds to get across to him.

'Oh Kit!' she burst out. ' I *am* glad to see you. Did you have a good term? When did you get home? All the others have got chicken-pox. Have you had it? I haven't, so Mum won't let me in to see Dan. It's been boring. Now Kate's got it too. . . .'

'Hold on!' Kit had to shout to get through her stream of words. He flicked his long dark hair out of his eyes, with the gesture that had become so familiar to the gang when they'd been hiding him, and turned to go home. Sarah skipped along beside him happily.

'I had a good term,' Kit told her. 'I still get lonely sometimes, but I've got some good friends now. And all the gang's letters helped. I'm in the under-twelve football team now, and we won most of our games this half term. I might make the cricket team next term. I must try to get some practice in with Dan and James.'

'Dan's got the pox!' Sarah reminded him cheerfully, 'but I'll bowl for you if the weather gets better. I don't think Dad'll let us play on the grass with it being so wet. It's hardly stopped raining for weeks here.'

'Has James got chicken-pox too?'

'No, he had it when he was about three. Jenny's got it, and Kate went home with it earlier today. Robert's had it, and has gone to be fed and fussed by Granny.' She pulled a face. 'I'm not allowed to visit the sick, because Mum doesn't want me to get it for the holidays. We've got the church holiday for the last week, after your parents come to get you, and if I get it now it'll spoil that. Have you had it?'

'Yes, I had it when we were living in Italy. It was so hot I couldn't bear it, and the maid kept sponging me down with cool water to stop the itching. All the time she jabbered on in Italian "povero bambino" and suchlike rubbish.'

Sarah laughed. Kit's life was so different from hers! Fancy having a maid looking after you when you were ill!

'What does "povero bambino" mean?'

'Poor baby!'

By the time they had swapped all the term's news, they were at the gate to 'The Old Orchard', the house where Daniel and Sarah lived, and which Kit was beginning to think of as his second home. Because his father travelled all over the world with his job, Kit had never stayed in one place for much longer than a year or two. Although he enjoyed travelling and living in foreign places with his parents, it was nice to feel that this house and this family would welcome him back whenever he wanted to come. Because Mr Masters, Sarah's dad, had dropped him off to meet Sarah straight from his school, Kit hadn't unpacked or seen Daniel, so he went along to the room he used when he stayed, and fished out his jeans and a sweatshirt. Once out of school uniform he felt much more comfortable, and went to knock on Daniel's bedroom door.

Daniel was in bed, feeling fed up and hot. His bed was littered with books and magazines that he'd tried to read and given up. He was covered in nasty raw looking bumps which itched dreadfully, and it was taking all his self control not to scratch them.

'I *hate* chicken-pox!' he announced as Kit walked in. Then his face broke into a wide smile as he saw who it was. 'Kit! I thought it was Mum coming in, or the doctor. When did you get here?'

'Your dad dropped me off outside school so I've just walked home with Sarah. He brought my stuff on in the car. I finished school at lunchtime today.'

'How long are you here for?'

'Ten days. Then Mother and Father are coming over, and we're going up north to see my grandfather, before we go off to Israel for a holiday. I get a whole month off school.'

'Lucky you. We only get two and a half weeks. Not that it's going to be much fun. I'm so fed up with being

9

ill and itchy.'

'Let's have a game of chess. It might make you stop thinking about the spots. I've got a small magnetic set. Wait, I'll go and fetch it.'

In a couple of minutes he was back, with the chess set and a small radio, which he switched on to some music.

'Bet I beat you. I'm champion of the Junior League.'

'No chance!' Daniel grinned. Perhaps being ill wouldn't be so bad now Kit was here.

2

Sarah's puppy

Sarah had two days of school left and each morning she set off feeling fed up. She'd so looked forward to Kit coming, and when he'd arrived he'd spent all evening in Daniel's room playing chess and swapping accounts of football matches. And now, she had to go to school, when just about everyone else was at home, and Daniel and Kit were having exciting times at home while she was doing maths and reading. It wasn't fair! She almost wished she had chicken-pox too. Then she remembered how ill Kate had looked before she went home, and how worried Mum had been about Daniel, and decided perhaps she didn't really want to be ill.

Only two more days till the end of term, she consoled herself. Those two days dragged. The weather was awful so they couldn't go out at playtime, or for games lessons. Kate wasn't there to talk to in class, and although Kit came to the school gate to meet her and walk home with her, after that he spent most of his time in Daniel's room. Sarah was not allowed to go in there in case she caught chicken-pox.

Daniel was over the worst now and his temperature was nearly back to normal, so he had been getting really bored in bed until Kit had arrived. Now, the boys had decided to make some models to go with Daniel's train set, so they were busy cutting and sticking. Kit came downstairs from time to time to fetch some more paper, or a particular coloured felt tip pen.

'Whatever are you doing? You must be making a complete town!' Sarah said, rather crossly once when he appeared. School had finished now, and she'd been looking forward to showing Kit all the artwork she'd done over the term. But he'd gone straight upstairs to Daniel.

'Not exactly!' Kit laughed. 'We are making several buildings though. It'll look really great when we've finished!'

'I thought you came to visit me, too,' Sarah muttered, half to herself. Kit heard, flicked his hair back, and gave her a long look.

'Sounds as if you're feeling jealous,' he commented, in an annoying grown up tone of voice. 'Of course I'm spending a lot of time with Dan. He's my friend and it's no fun being stuck in bed day after day, being ill. Besides, Jesus told us to look after people who aren't well or who are unhappy, didn't he? I'm only trying to follow what he'd do.'

Kit's calm reasonable tone made Sarah even crosser. She knew she was being unreasonable, but she was fed up with Daniel getting all the attention. Mum had been running round after him for a fortnight, and now Kit seemed to be doing the same! Besides, what made Kit think he had the right to preach to her? He'd only been following Jesus for a little while, and she, Sarah, had been a Christian for as long as she could remember.

'I don't care, anyway,' she threw at him as she flounced out. 'I don't want to play with silly boys anyway.'

Kit heard the back door slam behind her. He sighed. He hadn't meant to upset Sarah. I guess I did sound a bit goody goody, he thought. The truth is I was just enjoying what we're doing upstairs so much that I forgot Sarah might want some company too. Oh well. I'll try and make it up to her later. And he plodded upstairs with his bundle of card and paper.

Meanwhile, Sarah had made her way down the garden to the den. It was pouring with rain, and nearly dark, but the weather matched the way she was feeling, and anyway, it would be dry in the den. She crawled through the hedge at the end of the garden and went and sat on a pile of dry leaves under some thick rhododendron branches. Here it was quite dry.

The den was the gang's special place. Sarah and Daniel had discovered it the day they'd moved, almost a year ago now. At the bottom of their garden was a thick privet hedge, with room for agile children, or a slim adult, to crawl through near the bottom. The space on the other side of the hedge was cut off from the rest of the wood by a thick, almost impenetrable screen of rhododendron bushes. Daniel and Sarah and their friends who made up the gang, had had some lovely times in the den, having barbecues, sleeping out, and of course, keeping Kit hidden for nearly a week last year when he'd run away from home. During the Christmas holidays, they'd even had a barbecue surrounded by thick snow.

Now Sarah sat and hugged her knees, sheltered by the overhanging branches, but looking out at the damp, sad looking winter wood. Last summer seemed a long time ago.

I think Kit's changed. I think boarding school's changed him, she said to herself, but inside, she knew he hadn't; that it was she herself who was being selfish. I don't care. I'll find something to do without them tomorrow, she thought, but not even the thought that there was no school tomorrow cheered her up. I was so looking forward to these holidays, but now it's all spoilt. Rotten weather, selfish boys and Kate's ill too. Boring!

She sat there, determined to feel sorry for herself, as the daylight faded round her and the trees dripped. Gradually she became aware that a small insistent noise had been going on for a long time, unnoticed by her. She lifted her head to listen. What was it? Not a bird. An animal of some kind . . . . a small, frightened animal. It must be a puppy or a kitten lost in the wood, she thought, scrambling up.

She pushed her way through the wet bushes into the wood, and listened. Yes it was definitely in the wood not very far away. Sarah shivered. She'd come rushing out without putting her coat on, and now she was frozen from sitting still. The wood looked very dark too, and scary. From the den she could just see the lights from the house through the hedge, but in the wood it was completely dark. Shall I go back for my coat and a torch, she wondered. But then the whimpering noise came again, and she knew she couldn't leave it.

Carefully, slowly she tiptoed towards the sound. It was difficult to work out exactly where it was. There were so many other noises in the wood; leaves rustling, trees dripping and occasionally a bird screeched. Sarah stared through the semi darkness. Where was it? *What* was it?

Suddenly, underneath a clump of undergrowth, she thought she saw a movement. Crouching down, she left the path and moved slowly in that direction, pushing through the damp undergrowth, her skirt getting caught on rough twigs and brambles; peering through the darkness, trying to make her eyes see what was there. She was whispering gently to try to calm the frightened animal. Another movement – a small dark fluffy bundle wriggling backwards, away from her.

'Why, it's a puppy! Don't be afraid, little fellow, I won't hurt you. I've come to help you.'

Slowly, very slowly, she reached out her hand and held it agonisingly still, willing the little animal to trust her and come forward.

After what seemed hours, the whimpering stopped

14

and a little black nose reached hesitantly forward, sniffed her hand, and was jerked backwards again. Still Sarah waited, not daring to move, lest she should frighten the little animal away completely. Again the nose came forward, and sniffed, then a tiny pink tongue shot out and licked her finger.

Sarah giggled. 'That tickles!' The puppy whined, and licked her again.

Slowly, Sarah turned her hand so she could stroke the soft head. At first the puppy shrank away from her but at last it seemed to relax. Sarah shifted so she was sitting on the wet ground, and reached out two hands to pull it towards her. A set of sharp teeth sank into her thumb.

'You little horror!' she muttered, but she didn't let go. Holding it more firmly, she pulled it out of its hiding place, and cradled it on her lap.

'Oh, you poor thing!'

Now she could see that round its back legs was tangled a length of wire; that the poor little thing couldn't have run far away from her even if it had wanted to.

Sarah tried to untangle the wire, but she couldn't hold the puppy still with only one hand. He had stopped trying to bite her, but whenever she touched his back legs he wriggled and yelped, so Sarah gave up and sat there stroking him.

'You're beautiful!' she told him. 'I wonder what sort of dog you are.'

He had a thick woolly dark chocolate coloured coat, with black stripes running up from his nose to his ears and the top of his head. He had a paler creamy coloured patch under his chin, and a few white hairs on the tip of his tail. His face was short and triangular, almost like a cat's in shape.

'I think you must be a baby husky, or something like that. How did you get all tangled up in this wire? And how am I going to get you out of it?' Sarah scrambled to her feet, hugging the puppy against her chest.

'I'll have to get you safe in the den, and then go for Kit to help me.'

It was difficult scrambling through the bushes back into the den without dropping the puppy, but she managed it.

'Now, how can I keep you safe?' She looked round. There was a large plastic crate in the den, holding dry twigs and some charcoal left from the barbecues. Hastily Sarah kicked it over, and cradling the puppy under one arm, brushed the bits out of the crate. Then she gently put the animal into it. He immediately started to whimper again, and tried to scramble out.

'No. You've got to stay there. I know, you'd better have my jumper.'

She pulled it off, folded it and laid it in the bottom of the crate.

'There, little fellow, curl up on that.'

The puppy sniffed at the jumper, yawned a huge yawn, and lay down.

'Be good, I won't be long.' Sarah gave him a last pat, and then pushed her way through the hedge back into the garden. As fast as she could she ran back up to the house, through the kitchen and up the stairs to Daniel's room.

3

Sarah's secret

'Kit! Kit! Come out, you've got to help me! It's important!'

In the excitement of finding the puppy, Sarah had completely forgotten their quarrel. Kit, however, was still feeling a bit guilty about it, and he was surprised and pleased to hear her calling him.

'That's Sarah. I wonder what she wants.'

'Probably just some excuse to get you out of here.' Daniel didn't want Kit to go.

'No, it sounds important.'

By now Sarah was thumping on the door.

'Coming!' Kit called as he carefully disentangled himself from the model he was making.

'Hurry, Kit!' Sarah called. 'Bring some scissors or a knife with you.'

Kit grabbed up the scissors. As soon as he was outside the door, Sarah grabbed his hand and pulled him downstairs.

'Come outside. I'll tell you all about it then.'

Once outside, with the door safely closed, Sarah told Kit how she'd found the puppy, and how its legs were all tangled in wire.

'I tried to untangle it, but I couldn't do it alone. He wriggled so much and I was afraid of hurting him. I need you to cut the wire while I hold him still.'

'OK. What sort of puppy is he?'

17

'I don't know. He's tiny, but all fluffy and cuddly. I've never seen one like him before. Oh, I hope he's all right. I didn't want to leave him, but I didn't know what else to do.'

'Well, I think I'll go back and get a torch. We won't be able to see what we're doing without one. I won't be long; I've got one in my bag.'

'Hurry up then!'

While he was gone, Sarah worried about what she'd find when she crawled back into the den. Would the puppy still be there?

The back door opened, and Kit reappeared.

'Your mum said we're not to stay out long as we haven't got coats on,' he told her. 'I didn't tell her you haven't even got a jumper. Where is it, anyway?'

'Wrapped round the puppy – I hope! Come on!' and she grabbed Kit's hand and dragged him towards the den.

To Sarah's great relief, when she looked in the crate, the puppy was still there, curled up fast asleep, with the end of one of her jumper sleeves in his mouth.

'Oh, look, isn't he sweet!' she sighed.

Kit looked. 'I've never seen a puppy like that either. Poor little thing! I wonder how he got so tangled up. Let's get him sorted out.'

Sarah reached into the crate. The movement disturbed the puppy, for he opened his eyes, yawned, and when he saw Sarah, began to wag his tail.

'Look Kit, he knows me!' Sarah was delighted. As she lifted him out, he rubbed her hand with his head like a cat does, then licked it, then tried to bite it!

'No,' she said. 'That hurts!'

'Maybe he's hungry,' Kit suggested.

'Well, he's not going to eat me. You'll have to go and find something for him to eat when we've got the wire off.'

'Hold him still then, and I'll see what I can do.'

At first the puppy was nervous of Kit, but Sarah held him quite tightly, and talked soothingly to him, and very carefully, very gently Kit pulled and cut and untwisted the wire from his back legs.

'There, that's done,' he said at last. 'It doesn't seem to have hurt him too much. There's a couple of scratches, but nothing much. It's lucky his fur's so thick. I think that protected him a bit. Put him down and see if he stands all right now.'

'What if he runs away?'

'He can't get out of the den very easily. We'll catch him all right.'

So Sarah put the puppy gently down on the ground. He wobbled a bit at first, sat suddenly down and began to sniff at his back legs, then to chase his tail.

Sarah and Kit watched, entranced.

'He's beautiful!' Sarah dropped onto one knee and the puppy came bouncing across to her. 'A puppy of my own! A secret!'

'Do you mean to keep him then?' Kit asked, surprised. 'But he must belong to somebody. You can't just keep him!'

'I can!' Sarah retorted. 'He was probably tied up like that and dumped by someone who didn't want him.' She grinned at him. 'He'll be our secret. We'll make him a kennel out here in the den. No one else will know for a while because they're all ill. Then we can surprise them when they're all better. Till then, he's my puppy and our secret.'

Kit rather thought he ought to explain why this was not a very sensible plan, but it was so nice to be friends with Sarah again and to have their quarrel forgotten that he kept quiet. He'd always wanted a dog of his own too, but with his parents moving around so much that was quite out of the question. Besides, he didn't want to upset Sarah all over again, so he kept his doubts to himself, saying, merely, 'Well, we'll just have to keep our eyes open in the village in case he's lost. There'll be notices up if he is. . . . I'd better go and get something for him to eat, and some more warm things for him to sleep with.'

'Bring my hot water bottle,' Sarah suggested. 'It's on the floor by my bed, and if you can get it filled up without anyone knowing, we can put it in the crate and he'll be nice and warm.'

Kit pushed through the hedge and vanished. In a few minutes he was back again.

'I've got some bread and milk in here,' he said, handing Sarah a plastic box. 'And here's your bottle. I've wrapped it up in my games towel. I thought that wouldn't be missed.'

'Poor pet!' Sarah said to the puppy. 'Fancy having to sleep on Kit's smelly old games towel.'

'It's not smelly!' Kit burst out indignantly. 'They get washed once a week!'

Quite soon the puppy was settled in the crate again, with the towel-wrapped bottle under him, Sarah's jumper wrapped round him, and the box of soggy milky bread close to his nose.

'We'll have to go in, Sarah,' Kit reminded her. 'They'll get suspicious soon.'

'I know. I hope he'll be all right.'

'I'm sure he will. Baby animals sleep a lot. Look, he's asleep already.'

'I'll come down really early in the morning.' Sarah promised as she gave the puppy a last gentle stroke before she turned to push back through the hedge.

'Don't tell anyone about the puppy, will you; not even Daniel,' Sarah whispered as they reached the back door.

'How am I going to keep it secret from him?'

'You'll have to think of something. I want it to be a surprise.'

Once back inside the house, Sarah found she couldn't stop shivering. While she had been outside with the puppy she hadn't noticed how cold she'd got. Since she had pulled off her nice thick jumper without thinking, to give to the puppy, she'd been outside in just a cotton blouse for nearly an hour and she was chilled through.

Running upstairs to get a sweatshirt to put on, she met her mother, who took one look at her, and said 'Bath, young lady. I don't know what you were doing out in the den in this weather with no coat. Haven't I got enough to do with Daniel ill, without you catching pneumonia?'

And she marched Sarah off to the bathroom, where she spent the next half hour in a hot fragrant bubble bath.

Kit wandered slowly back to Daniel's room. As soon as he opened the door, Daniel demanded, 'What was all that about? Are you and Sarah friends again now?'

'Oh, it was just something she wanted help with. She's doing something in the den and needed an extra pair of hands, that's all.'

Kit's offhand manner didn't have the effect he'd hoped for. Daniel erupted!

'What? What's she doing out there without discussing it with me? It's *our* den, not just hers. Come on Kit, you've got to tell me.'

'No I can't.' Kit stood his ground. 'It's a secret and she asked me not to tell you. But it's nothing you won't approve of. It's quite exciting.'

Now it was Daniel's turn to feel left out.

'What is it? Do tell me. It's not fair leaving me out just because I'm ill. Will you be going out there again tomorrow?'

'Yes, I expect so. I don't really know. Come on, Dan,

we can do a bit more to this station building before bedtime.'

But Daniel was not interested in station buildings any more.

'You know, all the time I've been ill, I've been making plans for the den; things I want to do to it, and now you and Sarah are getting on and doing things without me. It's not fair.'

'I'll tell you as soon as Sarah says I can,' Kit promised him. 'But it's her secret. Anyway, it won't be long till you're out of bed, then you'll be down there with us. And I can promise that this won't make any difference to your plans at all. We'll still be able to do whatever you want.'

And no matter how Daniel pestered him, Kit refused to say another word about it.

Warm at last, tucked up in bed, Sarah was thinking about her puppy out in the den. She'd asked Jesus to look after him and told him she was sorry for getting cross with Kit. She decided to go to sleep really quickly so that she could wake up early and go out to the puppy, but sleep just would not come. No matter how firmly she shut her eyes, they soon seemed to pop open again, and thoughts kept crowding into her mind. How am I going to feed him? He can't just have bread and milk. How old is he? Should he be eating real dog food or special stuff? Will he be warm enough out there? What if a fox gets him? What kind is he anyway? What shall I call him? On and on, her busy mind went until at last she gave up trying to sleep, put the light back on and tried to read.

Half an hour later, when Mum popped in to say goodnight she found Sarah lying there, fast asleep, with the book under her head, and the light still on.

4

Meet Button!

When Sarah woke up the next morning, it was still very dark. She looked at her watch. Quarter to six! I must get up very quietly so as not to wake anyone, she thought. It took only a couple of minutes to pull on a warm track suit and her trainers, then she tiptoed to the door. As she pulled it open it creaked, and she held her breath, listening. No movement, so she carried on downstairs. She pushed open the kitchen door, and nearly jumped out of he skin when a quiet voice said 'Good morning, Sarah!'

'Oh Kit, how you scared me! I thought I was the only one awake.'

'I've been waiting for you for ages – at least two minutes!' Kit grinned. 'The rising bell at school goes at half past six so I'm used to getting up early. Let's go and see your puppy.'

Sarah opened the fridge door.

'What can we take him to eat? I don't think bread and milk's enough, do you?'

She scanned the shelves. There was some left over cooked liver on a plate. Sarah picked up a small piece.

'Yuk! I hate liver. Let's take some of this.'

'It's not my favourite either, but he might like it. Later on today, I can go to the shop and see if I can get a tin of special puppy food, if you like,' Kit offered. 'I've still got some of last term's pocket money left. That way your parents won't get suspicious.'

'Oh, would you, Kit? That'd be great. I've been wondering how we'll manage to feed him. I'll pay you back when I can.'

'That's all right.'

Kit always seemed to have enough money for what he needed. Sarah on the other hand, had to do jobs around the house for her pocket money and never seemed to have enough.

Outside it was very cold. They shivered as the damp air hit them. It was still quite dark and gloomy, though the cloud-covered sky did show signs of the coming day. Kit turned on the torch he had brought, careful to keep it pointed away from the house. As they came near the hedge that separated the garden from the den, Sarah clutched Kit's arm.

'What if he's not there? What if something's happened to him?'

'Do you want me to go in first and look?'

'Yes. . . . No. . . . I don't know. No, he's my puppy, I want to see him.'

And she pushed her way through the hedge first, with Kit close on her heels.

The puppy obviously heard them coming, as it began to make little yapping noises, and they could hear its claws scrabbling at the side of the crate.

'Hello, little one!' Sarah reached into the crate to pick him up. 'Look Kit, he's all right.'

Kit looked into the crate.

'Your jumper's not, though!' he commented grimly. 'Look!'

He held up the jumper; one sleeve was all frayed and chewed, and there was a milk stain on the front.

Sarah pulled a face. 'Oh dear, Mum'll be cross. I've only had that one a little while. Granny knitted it for me.' She shrugged. 'Oh well, since it's ruined he might as well keep it.'

The puppy was wriggling to get out of Sarah's arms, so she dropped him gently on the ground. Immediately he made little pouncing darts at the jumper Kit was holding, then got it between his teeth and began to shake it. Kit dropped it and they both dissolved into giggles as he played with it.

'I'm going to call him Button,' Sarah said suddenly. 'He's just the colour of a chocolate button and he's got a button nose.'

'Hello, Button!' Kit said solemnly. 'Pleased to meet you!'

Later that morning Kit set off to the village shop to buy some puppy food. He left Sarah in the den playing with Button. They'd gone back in for breakfast, and then immediately back out again, to the annoyance of Daniel and the surprise of Mrs Masters, who couldn't understand the attraction of the den in the rain! Button had been asleep, but had soon woken up, and begun chewing at a twig. Sarah dragged it along the ground, and he pounced and worried at it. Kit decided to leave then, while Button was awake, so Sarah wouldn't feel lonely in the den.

Daniel was feeling a lot better, but was still confined to bed, much to his disgust, with a promise of being allowed up in the afternoon.

Kit walked quickly through the wintry wood. As he went, he was remembering the adventure he'd had the previous summer. He passed the place where he'd fallen and broken his ankle. Now it looked completely different. Where the trees had been thick and leafy, now they were bare, and dripping with rain. The dry dusty paths had turned into mud tracks, and everywhere the ground was covered by soggy leaves. Even as Kit walked, the rain started again, and he pulled up his anorak hood and trudged on.

There were two shops in the village. The one he would normally have gone to, Bland's Stores, belonged to Robert's parents. Robert was one of the gang members, so Kit decided to play safe and go to the other one, where he was not so well known. If he bought a tin of dog food at Bland's he'd be sure to be cross-examined about who it was for! Mrs Bland always wanted to know everything about everyone!

It was further to the other shop, but Kit quite enjoyed the walk. It was nice after the regimentation of school, to do something on his own again. When he reached the shop he stopped to read the notices in the window, but there was nothing there about a lost puppy. Then he went inside and bought the puppy food, a football magazine for Daniel, and a box of chocolates for Mrs Masters, as a way of saying thank you to her for having him to stay.

As he came out of the shop, clutching his purchases in one hand and trying to get the change back into his jeans pocket with the other, two men went past. One knocked into him, shoving him with his elbow. The tin of puppy food slipped from Kit's arm and rolled across the pavement. The man growled, kicking the tin into the road with a booted foot. Kit stared; what a horrid man! It hadn't been his fault at all! He retrieved the tin and started homewards.

It was still raining when he crawled back through the bushes into the den. Sarah was sitting in the only dry place, with Button curled up asleep on her lap. She didn't look very happy.

'What's up?' Kit asked.

'He hasn't eaten any of the liver. He sniffed at it, bit a piece and then dropped it.'

'Well, maybe he doesn't like liver any more than we do. Sensible animal! We'll try him with this puppy food. Look, I'm just going to take these things in, and I'll bring Dan's penknife out so we can open the tin. I'm sure he'll eat some of it. Oh and I thought I'd ask your mum to take me to the library. I want to look up and find out what sort of dog he is. I'm dying to know, aren't you?'

Sarah nodded. She'd never seen a puppy quite like Button before. With the pointy ears, and squashed little nose, his face looked almost like a cat, but his body was definitely dog!

'I can tell her I need some books for a school project,' Kit continued. 'It's quite true; I do!'

'Shall I come too?' Sarah asked.

'Don't you think you'd better stay here with Button?'

'Yes, I suppose so,' Sarah agreed reluctantly. It was not turning out to be as much fun as she'd expected. It was cold and damp in the den, and all the puppy seemed to want to do was sleep.

At lunch time, Kit and Sarah found it quite difficult to keep their secret and yet still tell the truth.

'I can't understand why you want to be outside in this horrible weather!' Mum said.

'I don't get to see the den, except in the holidays,' Kit replied. 'It's been so long since I was here.'

'I know that, but couldn't you wait till the rain stops?' Mrs Masters asked.

Surprisingly, Sarah's dad spoke up for them. 'The rain won't hurt them. It's quite sheltered in that den. What are you doing out there; some sort of bird watching?'

'Not exactly,' Kit answered, 'but it is nature study. We're watching the animal life.'

Sarah giggled, and hastily changed it to a cough.

'No more of that, or you'll be confined to the house!' her mother said, looking worried. 'And if you do go out, make sure you're wrapped up warm.'

'I wondered if there would be any chance of you taking

27

me into town, Mrs Masters,' Kit said, changing the subject quickly, before Sarah's mum decided to ban them from going out at all. 'I need to get some books from the library for my holiday project.'

'I should think we could go this afternoon,' Mrs Masters said. 'I have to do some shopping, so I can drop you off at the library and pick you up later, when I've finished the shopping.'

This suited Kit fine, as it meant he'd have lots of time to research without being interrupted.

So after lunch, Kit and Mum set off for the nearest town, which was about eight miles away. Sarah dragged herself reluctantly back down the garden when they'd gone. It was cold, and she'd much rather have stayed indoors, especially as Daniel was out of bed and, curled up on the settee in the lounge, was watching a good film on television.

However, when she got down to the den, she found that Button had eaten all the food they'd left out for him and had tipped the crate over on to its side. As she came through the hedge he bounced towards her, giving little yaps of pleasure, and pushed his head at her legs just like cats do. Sarah laughed and bent down to stroke him. Button began to bite at her hair swinging forwards from her face.

Sarah hugged him.

'That's better, Button! You've decided to eat at last.'

She felt very relieved; it had worried her that the little animal hadn't eaten the liver, but now he looked so bright and full of energy that she stopped worrying and spent a happy hour playing with him. She trailed twigs along the ground, that he pounced on and then chewed up, they had tugs of war with her now completely ruined jumper, and rough and tumbles too. At last Button sat down and gave an enormous yawn. Grabbing the jumper with his teeth, he dragged it into the crate, and curled up on it. Another yawn, and he was fast asleep.

'Poor baby!' Sarah smiled at him. It was fun having a pet.

'I'm going to make you a run,' she told him. 'Now you've got the crate like that we really need somewhere where you can be kept safe, so you don't escape and get lost.'

She went back up the garden. In the garage she found a roll of chicken wire, and some canes. However when she got them back to the hedge she discovered the canes would go through all right, but the roll of wire wouldn't and she couldn't throw it high enough to go over the hedge into the den.

'Bother! What do I do now?'

Throughout her life, whenever Sarah had had a problem, she had always turned to Daniel. Being just sixteen months older than her, he had always been her friend as well as her brother, and although they had the usual quarrels, she could always rely on him for help.

Now she felt a bit guilty. It had been ages since she'd done more than shout through his bedroom door at him, because of the chicken-pox, and now, the first day he was allowed up, she'd left him alone in the house to come out here, ignoring his demands that she tell him what she was doing in the den. I'll go and tell him about Button and ask if he's got any ideas, she decided.

'Where have you been?' Daniel demanded, rather crossly, as she burst into the lounge. 'I thought you wanted to see this film.'

'I did,' Sarah replied, 'but I had something very important to do. Dan, I want your help, but you've got to promise to keep the secret.'

'Don't I always?' Daniel looked hurt.

'Yes, I know, but this one's really special. I've got a tiny baby puppy in the den!'

29

'A puppy? How? Where did he come from? Show me!'

Daniel was out of the chair and halfway to the door in a second.

'I found him in the woods, yesterday. You know when I had that row with Kit? Well, I went out into the den, and I heard this whimpering noise, and when I found it, it was Button. He was all tangled up in some wire. Kit came and helped me get him out.'

Already Daniel had his anorak on. Sarah followed him out of the back door. It was good to have Dan in on the secret. When they reached the hedge, it took only a moment for Daniel to throw the wire up and over the hedge. Sarah scrambled through, and pulled it down the other side. All this activity had woken Button up again, and he was romping round her feet, chewing her shoelaces, when Daniel came through the hedge. Button immediately dived for the crate and stood there, with his fur standing on end, hissing.

'Charming!' Daniel grunted. 'He seems really pleased to see me.'

'It's only 'cos he doesn't know you.' Sarah reached into the crate and picked Button up. Gently she brought him towards Daniel, who put out one hand so that the puppy could sniff it. Two sniffs, and then he gave a gentle nip.

'Ouch!' Daniel yelled. Sarah laughed.

'He did that to me too! I expect now you're his friend.'

'Wow! What a way to make friends! Isn't he sweet, though! What sort of dog do you think he is? I've never seen anything like him before.'

'I don't know. That's why Kit's gone to the library; to see if he can find out.'

'What are you going to do with him? You can't keep him a secret in the den for ever. He must belong to somebody; they might be looking for him. And we're

30

away on that holiday next week, don't forget.'

'I know. Kit and I are going to look out for "lost" notices in the village. But until someone says he's theirs, he's mine and I'm going to keep him! I don't expect Kate will be going on the holiday now she's got chicken-pox. I'll ask her to look after him then. And once he's a bit bigger and he's trained properly, perhaps Mum will let me keep him. I'll worry about that later, anyway.'

Daniel sighed. He knew from experience that Sarah never worried about things for long; she just expected things to turn out right; it was left to him to do the plotting and planning – and worrying!

5

He's a fox!

When Kit and Mum drew up in the car, back from their expedition into town, both Daniel and Sarah were sitting glued to the television, looking as if butter wouldn't melt in their mouths!

They had only just made it back into the house in time, and although he wouldn't admit it, Daniel was very tired after his busy afternoon. It was the first time he had been out of the house for over a fortnight, and he'd been working quite hard making the run.

He was pleased with the results though. They had made a nice big run for Button, and put the crate inside it, so now Sarah felt much happier about leaving him alone in the den. They'd refilled his food bowl and made sure he'd got some water to drink. The puppy had been playing around them all the time they were constructing his run, getting under their feet and chewing at the canes as they tried to push them into the ground, and generally holding up the work. Just before they'd finished he'd crawled back into his crate and curled up for a sleep.

Kit came bursting into the lounge, full of pent up excitement, and whispered. 'Come upstairs, Sarah, quick! I've got something to tell you.'

Safe in his room, Kit fished in his pocket and brought out a screwed up piece of paper.

'I did it in code in case your mum saw it!' he said proudly, handing it to Sarah.

Sarah took it and read. (The code was something the
gang had worked out the previous summer, and used
whenever they wanted to keep something secret. To
decode it, you had to add the top half of the capital
letters to what was printed. Since Kit often wrote his
letters to the gang from boarding school in code, they
had all had a lot of practice in decoding and could do it
quite easily now.)

ΠΕϽ ΙΝϽΙ Λ ϽϽϽ

ΠΕϽ Λ ΓϽΛ

'A fox! What do you mean? He can't be!'

'But he is, Sarah! Listen, I copied this out of a book:
"Fox cubs, when born, are covered in thick woolly chocolate brown or black fur, and lack the distinctive pointed
nose of the adult." There!'

'Wow, that does sound like Button,' Daniel, standing
just inside the doorway, breathed.

Kit had been too excited to notice him before. He
looked at Sarah, enquiringly. She nodded.

'I told him this afternoon. I was making Button a run
to keep him safe when we're not there. I couldn't do it
on my own.'

'Good, I'm glad we're all in this together, now. I was
looking forward to being part of the gang again. It did
seem as if, with this silly chicken-pox, we weren't going
to have any adventures. But now at least there's four of
us, with James, and Daniel back in action.'

'If I'm better, Jenny must be well on the way too; she
came out in spots the day after I did.'

'We can phone the vicarage and find out,' Sarah suggested. Kate, Sarah's best friend and Jenny her sister,
who was the same age as Daniel, were the vicar's daught-
ers, and had been Sarah and Daniel's first friends when
they had moved to their new house last year.

'Oh!' said Kit. 'I nearly forgot. I've got some other news for you. We might have a mystery to solve! I saw James in the library, and he was cross because he'd been shouted at in the wood by two men he'd never seen before. They told him he was on private property.'

'That's a load of rubbish!' Daniel interrupted. 'Everyone knows that wood is common land.'

'Yes, but it's strange, because I saw two strangers in the village this morning; they pushed me and growled at me for getting in their way, when I wasn't!'

'Do you think it's the same ones then?'

'Well, it seems a bit strange, doesn't it? Two lots of nasty men around all of a sudden? Not very likely! I wonder what they're up to?'

'Probably just staying somewhere,' Daniel said.

'If they're on holiday with the weather like it is, that's enough to make anyone grumpy.'

'Maybe!' Kit wasn't convinced.

Just then Mum called that supper was ready, so they had to go down.

'I'll tell you what else I found out about foxes later,' Kit whispered.

Next morning Sarah went down to the den before breakfast with a mug of milk for Button, that she had warmed in the microwave, because Kit had read in the book at the library that up until about six weeks cubs still took milk from their mothers. They guessed that Button was about a month old, because the book also said that until about a month fox cubs stayed in the earth, and after about that time their coats began getting paler, more like the ginger colour of adult foxes.

'There was a picture of a six week cub, and his nose was much more pointed too, so I think ours is very young,' Kit had said.

Button seemed to enjoy the milk. His little pink tongue flipped in and out at enormous speed. He hadn't eaten any of the food they'd left for him overnight, so Sarah threw it away and put out some fresh food. Watching Button eat the food, Sarah reached up absentmindedly to the hole in the tree where the gang put messages for each other. To her surprise there was a piece of paper there.

BE IN DEN AFTER CHURCH IMPORTANT NEWS. EVEN MORE SO NOW I SEE YOU'VE GOT A FOX. JAMES.

James must have come in on the tractor again. I wonder what he wants? she thought. James often got up very early to help his dad with the milking, and sometimes Mr Taylor gave him a lift into the village on the tractor, if he was going through. I must remember to tell the others, Sarah thought.

At half past ten they all went to church, except Daniel. Mum had decided that he looked tired and would be better staying at home. Daniel had agreed to keep an eye on Button for Sarah, so from time to time he ran through the rain to the den. Each time the fox cub was curled up, fast asleep, so Daniel didn't stay out long.

James and Jenny walked back from church with Kit and Sarah.

'It's so nice to be out again, even if it is raining,' Jenny said. 'I got so fed up with having chicken-pox. Poor Kate's just about at the worst stage now, but she hasn't got it very badly.'

It was Jenny's first time out since she'd gone down with it nearly a fortnight ago, and she had strict instructions not to be out long. They called in at the house for Daniel, and then ran on down the garden to the den to hear James' news, with a warning from Mrs Masters not to get so involved with gang business that they were all late for dinner! Jenny was absolutely enthralled by Button, who didn't do his usual trick of greeting her with a sharp nip from his pointed teeth, because he was fast asleep, and even the noise of the gang pushing through the hedge didn't wake him. So all Jenny could see was a tightly curled bundle of chocolate coloured fur half hidden by Sarah's jumper.

'What's all the mystery about, James?' Daniel enquired.

'I came to tell you to look out for orphaned fox cubs in the wood, but it seems I'm too late. Yesterday evening Dad found a vixen that had been shot. She'd obviously dragged herself around quite a bit, till she died, and was in a dreadful state. Dad was furious.'

Kit was puzzled. 'But I thought your Dad didn't like foxes. He keeps dogs to chase them away.'

'He doesn't want foxes near the farm buildings, because of the chickens, sure, but he can't stand cruelty to animals. Our dogs only chase, they never hurt. Dad says this was a deliberate act of cruelty. Whoever did it must have known she was hurt, but not killed, and instead of shooting again to kill her outright, they just left her to bleed or starve to death.'

Sarah shuddered. Having lived in the country for a while, she knew that lots of people saw foxes as vermin, but also she knew that the local people would not cause any animal unnecessary suffering.

'Why would anyone do that?' she asked.

She leant over to lift Button out of the crate. As she did so he opened one eye, licked her hand with his tiny tongue, then snuggled down in her arms and went back to sleep.

'It gets worse,' James said grimly. 'The vixen was lactating.'

'What on earth's that?' Kit interrupted. Sarah was glad he'd asked because she didn't know either.

'She was producing milk. It means she was feeding babies,' James explained. 'Anyway Dad followed the trail of blood back a bit, to see if he could find the cubs, and he found a dead one. It looked as if it had followed its mum, stayed with her when she died, and just starved to death.'

'So do you think ours is one of hers too?' Kit asked.

'It's got to be, hasn't it?' James replied. 'It's the right age and everything. How did you find it?'

So once again Sarah launched into the story of how she'd found the fox.

James listened carefully. When she finished he said, 'Well, it looks as if yours had a lucky escape.'

'Why would anyone want to kill a whole family of foxes?' Sarah puzzled, stroking Button's fur where he lay curled up asleep on her lap. 'How could anyone kill something like Button?'

6

The investigation begins

The gang were silent as they mulled over the sad news James had brought them. Then suddenly Daniel burst out, 'It's a mystery for the gang to work out! It's just what we need for the holidays! We can get Kate thinking about it too, it'll give her something to do while she's confined to home. It's dreadfully boring having chicken-pox. We'll try and work out who did it and what the motive could be.'

He pulled out the little notebook that he always carried round in his pocket.

'Now, where do we start?'

'Farmers!' Kit said. 'They have a motive.'

James flared up in defence of his father and friends.

'No farmer would do that!'

'We have to investigate every possibility, no matter how unlikely it looks,' Daniel said, importantly. 'That way we can eliminate the innocent ones. Can you ask around the farms to find if anyone knows anything?'

James nodded and Daniel wrote a note in his book – 'James to investigate farmers.'

'Who else might have done it?' Sarah asked. 'What about the hunt?'

'They shouldn't be meeting this time of year. They're not allowed to hunt when there are likely to be baby cubs,' Jenny told her. 'I think we can definitely rule them out.'

'Anyway, they use hounds, and horses, don't they, not guns?' Kit chipped in.

Silence fell, as they all tried to think of someone else who might have shot the fox.

'Let's ask around in the village. There's the two shops, and the post office,' Kit suggested. 'I don't mind doing that.'

Sarah shuddered; she thought Kit was very brave; she didn't like talking to strangers. It was odd how Kit never seemed to mind. I suppose it's having lived in so many different places, Sarah decided. He's spent his life getting to know new people.

'What will you say?' Sarah asked Kit.

'I'll say we've heard that there have been some dead foxes found, and ask if they can tell me any more about it.'

Daniel wrote down 'Kit – shops' in his book.

'I'll see if I can find any clues in the wood itself,' Daniel said. 'What about you, Jenny?'

'I'll see if Dad has any ideas. He talks to lots of people so he might have heard something.'

Daniel added these two ideas to his list.

'What shall *I* do?' Sarah asked. She didn't want to have to face strangers and ask questions.

Daniel noticed she was looking worried, so he said,

'Would you mind being stationed at base? We'll need someone here to report back to. You'll need to be here quite a lot of the time anyway because of Button. I'll leave you the notebook and you can write up our findings.'

'Great!' Sarah beamed. 'I think now we should write a note to Kate for Jenny to take. Then we can start tomorrow.'

'When shall we meet up again, then?' James asked.

'When we've got time we'll go and do our investigations,' Daniel said. 'We can each report back to Sarah, and have a gang meeting on, let's say Wednesday straight after lunch to see how we're getting on. If we need one sooner, we'll phone round. Sarah can do that. Now let's get this letter done.'

It took quite a long time to work out what they wanted to say, and then to get it into code, but at last it was done.

KATE

TWO DEAD FOXES

FOUND IN WOOD.

SUSPICIOUS. ONE SHOT.

ONE STARVED. GANG

INVESTIGATING ANY

IDEAS REPORT TO GANG

VIA JENNY

Daniel handed it over to Jenny. Just at that moment Button woke up. He opened his bright, brown eyes, then, yawning widely, slid off Sarah's lap and began to attack her shoes. The gang spent a few minutes playing with the cub, before they went their separate ways for lunch.

The great investigation started on Monday morning. Sarah, Daniel and Kit went down to the den after breakfast. Sarah had already been down for her early morning visit to Button, with some milk, and he'd wolfed the whole lot down, though he hadn't eaten any of the puppy food. Kit decided to go and do his research in the village, leaving Daniel and Sarah to play with Button.

'Will you get some more puppy food?' Sarah asked.

'We've nearly finished this tin.'

'Is it worth it? We've thrown most of it away, haven't we? I don't think Button's eaten more than about half what we've given him.'

'Try a different make,' Daniel suggested.

'Good idea! I'll see what I can find.' And Kit pushed his way through the bushes into the wood, using it, as the gang so often did, as a short cut into the village.

Left behind in the den, Sarah shuddered.

'I hope Kit doesn't meet those horrid men again! James saw them in the wood.'

'He'll be all right,' Daniel assured her. 'He knows to keep away from them if he does meet them, and anyway, the weather's so awful, nobody's likely to be about.'

It was true. Before breakfast, when Sarah had been out, it had been grey, but dry; now a steady drizzle had set in. In fact they had had some difficulty persuading Mum that they really did need to go out. At last, as he so often managed to do with adults, Kit had succeeded in convincing her of his viewpoint – in this case, that the fresh air would do them good, even if it was raining. Mum had insisted on gloves and wellies as well as anoraks, but she had given in and let them out.

In the den, under the overhanging branches, they were sheltered from the rain, but the whole atmosphere felt damp, as if the rain had soaked into the air and stayed there, like in a sponge. On Button's fur, drops of moisture were collecting, giving a greyish sheen to his dark coat. He just sat in the rain, not bothering to shake it off, staring towards the wood.

'Does Button often sit still like that?' Daniel asked suddenly. He'd only seen him full of bounce before, or fast asleep.

'No, he's usually much more lively. Maybe he's fed up with the rain too.'

'He might be missing his mum.'

'Or his brothers. Poor Button!' And Sarah reached over the wire of the enclosure they had made, picked him up and cuddled him to her. Usually when she held him tight he endured it for a few minuteus, then wriggled and bit till she let him go, but this time he just snuggled closer, and in a little while was fast asleep.

'We might as well put him back in his crate to sleep and go indoors out of this rain,' Daniel suggested.

Sarah nodded. There was not much point staying out here to keep Button company if he was asleep and she was getting soaked through, and cold with standing still, so she carefully lowered Button into the crate and covered him with her jumper. Then the two of them ran back through the rain into the warmth and comfort of the house.

In the village, with his tape recorder, Kit had put on his polite grown-up voice, which always charmed people into giving him what he wanted. He had decided to ask people if they would mind giving him an interview about things that went on in the village, and gradually get them round to the subject of the foxes.

In Bland's Stores it went very well, because Robert's mother knew him and liked the gang members. She told him all about the chicken-pox epidemic, and how she'd had to send poor Robert away to his Granny's to get his strength back, and how sad Robert would be to have missed seeing Kit and how the shop wasn't doing so well, because in the bad weather people got their cars out and went to the supermarket in town rather than walking to the village shop. Kit felt a bit guilty at this, and glad that she didn't know that's where Mrs Masters had been going the previous afternoon when she'd dropped him off at the library.

When he tried to lead the subject round to foxes, she shrieked, 'Don't talk to me about foxes! Nasty vicious creatures. Should be put down, all of them. Besides they carry diseases.'

Then, changing the subject without even taking breath, so that it took Kit a little while to realise what she was talking about, 'Here, I've got lots of these new muesli bar things, and this kind aren't selling too well. Could the gang use them?'

'Thank you very much, Mrs Bland. That's very kind. We're always hungry you know,' Kit said.

So Mrs Bland added a large packet of crisps to the bars.

Just then another customer came in, so Kit beat a polite retreat before she could start again.

'Thank you very much indeed, Mrs Bland. That was a very interesting interview; very kind of you. I'll go now as you have a customer. Thank you again.'

As he closed the door behind him he could hear Mrs Bland in full flow again, telling the unfortunate customer all about Robert's friend who had to do a report for 'that posh boarding school he goes to.'

Smiling to himself, he added a comment to his recording, 'It sounds as if she's got the motivation, but can you imagine Mrs Bland knowing how to use a gun? Anyway, she's too kind hearted. No further forward on the investigation, but emergency rations are certainly well stocked up now. On to the Post Office!'

The Post Office was busy, so all Kit got there was a short moan about people who didn't have the right change when they came in for stamps, and a comment that the bad weather made the postman's job very unpleasant. The lady behind the counter didn't know anything about the dead fox, and couldn't think of any other news, telling Kit that 'this is such a sleepy village nothing ever happens here.'

In the other shop, Kit had more luck. The shop was empty, and the assistant obviously bursting with news.

'There's been a robbery! Didn't you know? Mrs

Potter, who lives in that thatched cottage by the bus stop; you know the one I mean? Well, she came in here earlier today in a dreadful state. She'd popped in next door to her neighbour, old Mr Merritt, because he's not been too well and can't go out in this cold weather. So she'd just popped in to make sure he was all right, and to see if he wanted her to do any shopping for him. She couldn't have been gone more than ten minutes, she said, and when she got back, all her silverware had gone off the mantelpiece. All young Joanne's swimming cups, and her husband's cricket cup, and her silver teapot that was her mother's; all gone! Of course she had the police round, but what can they do? In a terrible state she was, when she called in here. It's dreadful, isn't it? Things like that just don't happen in our village!'

Walking back through the wood, Kit replayed his tape. I wonder if that's another mystery the gang should be working on, he thought. I'll suggest it to Sarah when I get back.

7

Daniel's discovery

After lunch it was Daniel's turn to go out and investigate. He'd decided to survey the wood, looking particularly for any other dead fox cubs, as it seemed highly unlikely that the litter had consisted of only two. He also wanted to see if he could find the earth they had come from. He knew this would be difficult, because foxes are very good at finding really secret places, but he was going to have a go. Mum had only agreed to him going out at all if he was really well wrapped up and didn't stay out in the rain too long.

Kit had a school project to do over the holidays, so he settled down to that.

Sarah decided to start making notes from Kit's recordings of the morning's discoveries, before going out to the den again to play with Button. After about half an hour she packed up her writing things and went down to the den. She took a groundsheet to sit on, a blanket to wrap in, and a book to read. Sarah dropped her bundle, then bent down to look at Button. He was asleep again, making little whimpering noises in his sleep and breathing very fast. I hope he's all right, she thought. She contemplated picking him up, but then decided that would wake him, so she left him there and, laying her groundsheet out, she curled herself up in the blanket, opened her book, and started to read.

Sarah had been up very early for three days now, to

come down to the den to Button, and she hadn't been sleeping very well either, because of worrying about waking up early. So now it wasn't long before her eyes closed, and she wriggled down further into the blanket. A few minutes later, she too was asleep.

Daniel walked quickly through the wood. He'd decided to start at the road side, and work back towards the den, looking for any clues he could find. It wasn't really a very big wood, and by now he knew all the paths in it fairly well. There was the path the gang members used most often, leading from the village to the den, with several smaller side paths off it. The way to the den was actually one of these side paths, as the main path curved round and led to the far end of the wood, out towards the country. It was only James who came that way.

Daniel wandered up and down the paths, but there didn't seem to be anything out of the ordinary, until he turned down a little winding path he couldn't remember ever having been down before. Suddenly he stopped, and stared at the muddy ground beneath his feet. How strange! Why all those footprints? Intrigued, he followed the tracks to the end of the path. It didn't go anywhere! It just came up to a steep bank where there were tree roots showing, and a lot of soggy wet leaves meant he couldn't see the footprints anymore. He turned and began to follow them back towards the main path again. Soon after the two paths joined, the ground was covered with fallen leaves again, so he couldn't see which way the footprints went.

Puzzled, Daniel turned back towards the den. I'll see what Kit thinks, he decided. It's certainly odd, that many footprints in the wood. We hardly ever see anyone walking through.

Back in the den, Sarah was still asleep. She woke with a jump when Button barked a sharp little yap at Kit pushing his way through the hedge. She sat up and stretched.

'Oh, I'm stiff!' she yawned. 'I must have been asleep all afternoon.'

'No, Dan's only been gone about an hour,' Kit told her, 'I finished my project so I came out to see how you were getting on. You must have been very tired.'

Sarah yawned again. 'I was! I feel awful now though. My arm aches.'

Kit dropped down onto the groundsheet beside Sarah and peered in at Button, who had curled up again in his crate.

'Is Button all right?' he asked. 'His fur looks rather dull and flat; not fluffy like it was.'

Sarah looked. It was true. Where Button's fur had been woolly and fluffy it now looked rather bedraggled and, yes, somehow dull.

'I think so,' she said. 'He's not eaten much though. And he's been asleep nearly all day. Do you think we're feeding him right?'

'I don't know.'

They looked at each other. Suddenly the excitement of the adventure was forgotten in their worry over this little fox cub.

'It would be awful if he got ill and died too!' Kit said, thinking aloud. 'Whoever it was has already killed at least two foxes.'

Sarah reached in and grabbed Button. Clutching him to her, she announced, 'Well, he's not going to die. They're not going to have killed Button too. I'm looking after him and he's going to be all right.'

She looked so fierce, that, despite his worry about the little animal, Kit laughed.

'Yes, I'm sure he is. I expect he's just getting used to being on his own. Try him with some more of the puppy food.'

Sarah put Button down, and spooned out some food from the tin. Button sniffed it, took two mouthfuls, and then sat back and whined.

'Come on, Button,' Sarah pleaded, 'You've got to eat something.'

'I'll go and get him some warm milk,' Kit said. 'He drank that last time.'

Sarah sat waiting for Kit to come back, holding Button, and worrying. Lord Jesus, please make Button be all right, she prayed. What else can I do for him? I do want him to be all right. I do love him.

When Kit came back with the milk, Button drank most of it, and immediately seemed more lively so they spent a little while playing with him.

'I think I'll go through and see if I can find Dan,' Kit said, after about twenty minutes.

Sarah nodded. 'Fine!' she said. So Kit left her playing with Button and made his way into the wood.

Button had found a fir-cone and was pretending it was a mouse. He threw it into the air with his front paws, watched where it rolled when it landed, and then stalked it. With his nose almost to the ground, and his bottom and tail stuck up, he wriggled on the spot then suddenly jumped onto the fir-cone, only to start the whole game over again. Sarah watched delightedly. He really did seem to be a cross between a cat and a dog; she'd seen the cats on James' father's farm doing exactly the same thing with real mice!

Button soon got tired again and curled up in Sarah's arms. Feeling a bit happier about him, she tucked him up in the crate, with her very holey jumper wrapped round to keep him warm. Then she went back indoors to warm up and wait for the boys to come back.

Kit had met Daniel not far from the den, and together they had retraced their steps to the little path Daniel had found.

'Over here, Kit!' Daniel said. 'What do you make of this? Look, see here. There are lots of footprints in the mud.'

'Well, the gang comes and goes a fair bit through this wood,' Kit remarked reasonably, switching his tape recorder onto 'play' as he did so.

'Yes, but these are too big to be our footprints. See!' And Daniel fitted his own shoe into the nearest print. Sure enough there was room to spare at the toe end.

'Well, I don't see why other people shouldn't be allowed to walk in the woods. They're not private after all!'

'No . . . but we've never seen this many prints before, and we hardly ever meet anyone in the wood. It doesn't lead from anywhere to anywhere apart from our house. Besides, these prints don't go anywhere. I've followed them. Look.'

And the two of them began to follow the footprints. They came to the steep bank and stopped. On the bare mud above the bank there were no more footprints.

'So they came here, looked at the view, then turned round and went back,' Kit said. 'So what?'

'Fine if it was only one or two tracks, but there's at least three lots coming and going. And anyway, why come here to look at the view?'

Kit looked. 'Hmm, I see what you mean.'

There really was no view! Beyond the bank, which raised the ground level by nearly two metres, all that could be seen were wet trees and tangled brambles.

'What's your theory, then?' Kit asked Daniel.

'I don't know yet, but I think it looks suspicious. We'll keep an eye on it. I'll come out every day to see if there are more footprints.' Daniel replied thoughtfully. 'Anyway, we'd better get back. I promised Mum I wouldn't be out too long this afternoon. I think she's getting a bit suspicious at the way we all keep disappearing into the den. We'll have to be careful.'

8

What's wrong with Button?

When Sarah ran down to the den first thing the next morning, it was raining harder than ever. Button was curled up under the jumper in the crate, fast asleep, so Sarah poured the milk she'd brought into his bowl and raced back up to the house. Seeing her wet hair at breakfast, Mum got cross, and told all three children that they were not to spend hours out in the den in the rain again today; they were to have a bit more sense and stay indoors in the warm. On the whole they obeyed her! Sarah and Kit took it in turns to dash down to check on Button, but he spent most of the day asleep anyway, so they felt quite justified in not staying long.

'I don't think he likes the rain either!' Sarah said once, looking at the water streaming down the window pane. 'It hasn't let up for hours.'

'As soon as it does,' Daniel announced, 'I'm dashing out to check how many footprints there are in the wood.'

'Oh Dan, don't be silly! Do you really think those silly footprints are significant?' Sarah asked.

'I'm sure they are!' Daniel flared back at her. It was all set to develop into one of those squabbles that nobody intends but that always seem to happen on days when you are cooped up indoors and would really rather be outside doing something else, but Kit stopped it. Flipping through the Radio Times, he noticed that there was a film coming on that they all would enjoy. So they settled down in front of the television. After the film, Daniel dashed out to check on Button and look at the mysterious footprints

'I told you they're important!' he announced triumphantly when he arrived back. 'There's more than there were before.'

'I wonder what they mean, then? Do you have any idea?' Kit asked.

'No, but I'll keep on till I do,' Daniel said.

After tea the phone rang. Sarah answered it; it was Jenny, ringing to say that she had some news, which might be useful.

'I'll come round tomorrow afternoon,' Jenny said, 'but Mum says it's got to be in the house, not out in the den, if it's still raining, and I'm not to stay long.'

Sarah reported this to the two boys who were playing chess by the fire in the lounge, and then ran out to check on Button before she went to bed. He was still fast asleep, so she left him there, and went into write her report of the day's happenings in Daniel's notebook.

She went to bed feeling quite pleased with herself, breathed a quick prayer for Kate, still in the uncomfortable itchy stage of chicken-pox, and for Button out in the dark. Then she fell fast asleep.

Meanwhile, Daniel had decided to ring James, to tell him to be there the next day too.

'Good!' Kit was pleased. 'We'll be nearly all the gang together again. Only Kate and Robert missing.'

The gang was very important to Kit. While he'd been travelling around with his parents, he hadn't made many friends, and it was really only last summer that he'd realised for the first time what fun it was to be part of a group of children doing things together. The holiday they'd all had after that disastrous running away, had meant they'd all got to know each other really well. It was only the thought of the gang, and their friendly letters, that had helped him cope with the first few lonely weeks at boarding school, when everything had been so strange and difficult. So he looked forward to the school holidays when they could all be together, and like Sarah, he had been bitterly disappointed when it had seemed that the chicken-pox would spoil everything.

The next day, when the gang assembled in Kit's bedroom, because it was furthest away from the stairs, and therefore they were less likely to be overheard, Sarah and Kit were worried again. They had been out to the den before breakfast, and several times during the morning. Each time they'd tried to get Button to drink some more milk, or have a little bit of the puppy food. Each time he had taken a little bit, but not much, and hadn't wanted to play at all, just crawled straight back into his crate. His fur was all dull and matted still, and his nose was hot and dry. Sarah knew that in a dog, this meant they weren't well, but neither of them knew if the same applied to a fox. So it was a rather preoccupied Sarah who prepared to take notes.

'What's the news, then, Jenny?' Daniel demanded, when they were all settled and the door firmly closed.

'It's just that I heard Dad talking early yesterday evening. It seems there have been several robberies in the village over the last couple of days.'

'We already know about one. The woman in the shop told me. Mrs Potter's lost her swimming cups,' Kit said.

'Not exactly; they're Joanne's!' Jenny corrected him, smiling. 'Yes, that's one. And last night, the churchwarden's wife came in to tell Dad that they've been broken into and lost a lot of jewellery, and Dad said that the house down the road from us has had jewellery and cameras taken. All within the last couple of days.'

'Does your Dad have any idea about who might have done it?' James asked.

'No, except he doesn't think it's anyone from the

village. He asked Kate and me if we'd seen any strangers around.'

'I have!' Kit said. 'Those two horrible men who pushed me outside the shop the other day.'

'I wonder if they're the same ones I saw in the wood?' James said. 'What did they look like, Kit?'

'Youngish, scruffy jeans and greasy sticking up hair. One of them had a leather jacket on.'

'Mmm, it sounds like the same ones. I wonder why they were in the wood.'

'Perhaps they just didn't want anyone to see them and the wood seemed a good place to hide,' Jenny suggested. 'What did they do when they saw you, James?'

'They told me to get out because the wood was private! I wonder . . . do you think they might be the robbers?'

'I wonder if it's their footprints!' Daniel said. 'It could be, couldn't it?'

'I thought we were trying to investigate who killed the foxes!' Sarah interrupted, crossly. 'Do I have to start a new page for robbers now?'

Sarah's outburst was so unusual that Daniel and Jenny both looked at her in consternation.

'What's up, Sarah?' Jenny asked gently.

Sarah just sat there. She didn't want to say anything, because she knew if she did she'd probably cry, and once she'd started she wouldn't be able to stop.

'She's worried about Button,' Kit explained for her. 'He's not eating properly, and we're worried that he's not well.'

'We ought to get the vet to look at him, then, didn't we?' Practical Jenny had put her finger on the solution.

'But I'll have to tell Mum, then,' Sarah wailed, 'And she won't let me keep him, and I did want him to be my pet.'

'But if you love him, and he's not well, you've got to get someone who knows what to do, haven't you?'

Jenny's calm gentle voice went on. 'Loving something means doing what's best for them, doesn't it?'

Sarah sighed. Sometimes Jenny was just too good and sensible. But she knew Jenny was right. Inside herself she already knew that she would have to get help for Button, if he didn't perk up, but she'd been trying to convince herself he would be all right.

'I'd better go and tell Mum, and get it over with,' she said, brushing her tears away, and standing up. 'She's going to be cross.'

'I'll come with you.' Kit stood up and flicked his hair back from his face. 'I'm in it just as much as you are.'

Sarah smiled him a grateful smile. 'Thanks, Kit!'

'Let's go then. Out to execution.' Kit grinned. 'It won't be that bad, Sarah. Your mum's really nice. The rest of you might just as well get on with solving the mystery without us. Come on, Sarah.'

9

Poor Button

Left behind, Daniel, James and Jenny looked at each other.

'Poor Sarah!' Jenny said at last. 'Do you think he's really ill, Dan?'

'He doesn't look too good. He's sleeping an awful lot more than he did at first and he's not eating much,' Daniel told her. 'It's too young really to have left its mother, I think. I didn't realise she was that worried though.'

'Do you really think it's one of the dead vixen's cubs then?' Jenny asked.

'It's got to be,' James replied. 'Sarah found it all tangled up in some wire. If it had run in panic it could easily have got tangled up like that. Dad found the dead vixen the next morning, with another cub nearby. It all fits!'

'What about these two strange men? And the footprints? When did they appear?' Daniel thought maybe there was some connection between them and the dead fox but at the moment he couldn't see what.

'I saw them the same day Sarah got her fox,' James said. 'I think Kit bumped into them the next day.'

'Do you really think there's some connection then, between the dead foxes and the robberies?' Jenny asked. 'It doesn't seem likely to me.'

'No, maybe not,' Daniel agreed. 'But you've got to

admit that it's odd the two things happening at the same time.'

'I wonder where the two men are living. Maybe they had some good reason to be in the wood. Maybe they're not baddies at all.'

James laughed.

'Oh Jenny, you're always ready to believe the best of people. But if you'd seen them, you'd think they were bad, too!'

'They might be on the caravan site!' Daniel suggested. 'Is it open at this time of year, James?'

'I don't think so. I'll ask Dad,' James answered. 'I'd better be off now anyway. Mum said to be sure to get home before dark.'

Daniel stood up as well.

'I'll come out with you now. I want to have another look at those footprints in the wood. I'm sure they're suspicious, but I can't quite work out how yet.'

I think I'll hang around to see how Sarah and Kit get on,' Jenny said. 'Will that be all right, Dan?'

'Sure! Sarah will be glad to have you around if she's got to give up the fox. Can you make some notes about what we've decided? Sarah was doing it.' He passed her the notebook. Jenny started writing.

Sarah and Kit had gone downstairs to find Mrs Masters. Sarah was trying hard not to cry.

'Tell you what!' Kit said, having stolen a sideways look at her sad face, 'Shall we just go down and see what he's like now? If he's all bright and bouncy again, we won't bother telling your mum, but if he still looks ill, we will. Agreed?'

'OK,' Sarah didn't really expect him to be better, but it was worth a try.

So instead of saying anything to Mrs Masters, who was in the kitchen making a pie, they ran quickly out and down the garden. Behind them, Mrs Masters shouted at them to put coats on, but they ignored her and ran on. When they got into the den, it was obvious immediately that Button was not any better. He didn't give his usual little yap of welcome, nor did he come bounding out of the crate to greet them. Instead, he just lifted his head, gave a little whine and one sad thump of his tail.

'Oh, Kit, we'll have to go and ask Mum to ring the vet. He's getting worse. Come on.' And she scrambled back through the hedge.

Sarah burst in through the back door, with Kit following close behind, and flung herself at her mother.

'Mum, we've got a baby fox in the den and I think he's dying so will you ring the vet please,' she sobbed.

Mrs Masters looked across at Kit.

'What's all this about, Kit?' she asked.

'Sarah found a baby fox cub in the wood a few days ago,' Kit explained, 'and she's been keeping it in the den. We think its mother is the one that Mr Taylor found shot. Anyway, it doesn't seem to be very well, and it's getting worse. We'd like you to phone the vet to come and have a look at it, please.'

Mrs Masters put Sarah gently away from her, washed and dried her hands, and took out a large empty cardboard box from the bottom of the cupboard.

'Come on, let's go and have a look at him. We'll put him in here and bring him up to the house. Then I'll phone the vet.'

By now it was raining again. Sarah pushed through the wet hedge first, then Kit, then last, with rather more pushing and shoving, Mrs Masters. Button was awake, and gave a little yap. Sarah dropped onto her knees beside the crate.

'Oh Button, you're better!' she cried. But when she looked at him, she could see he wasn't really. His little pink tongue reached out and licked her hand, and it was hot. So was his nose, and very dry.

Mrs Masters knelt down beside Sarah and reached out to pick him up.

'Come on little fellow!' she said gently. Button waited till her hands were really close, then lunged forward and sank his sharp little teeth deep into her thumb. Mrs Masters gave a yelp of pain.

'Oh Button!' shouted Sarah and Kit together. Button, frightened by all the noise, shrank back into the corner of his crate, and cowered there, snarling.

'I've never seen him behave like that before,' Kit said.

'I'm sorry, Mummy. Did he hurt you?' Sarah asked.

'Not much. He's only frightened. Sarah, you try to calm him and then pick him up. See if you can get him through the hedge and into the box.'

Slowly, Sarah began to stroke the frightened cub, crooning quietly to him all the time. At last he relaxed and crept forward. She picked him up and stood up, cuddling him against her. Kit picked up the jumper, and crawled through the hedge to lay it in the bottom of the box. Sarah went next. It was not easy to get through without letting go of Button, but at last she managed it and lowered him into the box. He immediately grabbed the jumper between his teeth, and turned round and round with it. When he had it as he wanted it, he lay down. Kit picked up the box, and they began to walk back up the garden to the house.

'Where shall I take it, Mrs Masters?'

'Into the kitchen, I think,' Sarah's mum replied. 'I think maybe he's a bit chilled. Usually he would have been warm and snug underground with his brothers and sisters, during the bad weather. It's a pity you didn't trust me, and tell me about finding him, Sarah. Still, it's too late now to worry about that. Put him down in the corner, and stay with him while I go and ring the vet.'

Once indoors, Mrs Masters went first to the tap and rinsed her hand. Where Button had bitten her there were pinpricks of blood.

'Oh, Button, you were naughty!' Sarah whispered. 'Why did you do that?'

'I'll go and put some cream on this, then make that phone call,' her mum said.

A few minutes later she was back again.

'The vet's calling in on his way home from surgery. He'll be about an hour. I'm trusting you to look after Button till then, Sarah. I don't want him running wild all round the house.'

Sarah sat down on the floor beside the box. Button was standing up peering over the edge, his little black nose twitching as he sniffed the interesting kitchen smells.

'Can I give him some milk, Mum?' Sarah asked.

'I'll do it!' Kit offered, thinking that if Sarah moved the cub would probably jump out of the box to follow her. 'You stay there, Sarah.'

Button drank most of the milk, then gave himself a good wash and curled up to go to sleep. Kit had vanished upstairs, to find out what the others were doing, and in a few minutes, he reappeared with Jenny.

'Jenny's the only one still here,' he told Sarah. 'The others have gone out investigating. Jenny's written up the notebook for you. She wants to wait with us for the vet.'

'Can I?' Jenny asked. 'It won't frighten Button?'

'No, he's asleep!' Sarah said. 'Come and look.'

So Jenny came and knelt down beside Sarah.

'He's so beautiful!' she whispered. 'I didn't know foxes could be that dark brown colour. I thought they were all ginger.'

'According to the book I found in the library they're all born like this,' Kit said. 'The colour changes as they grow up.'

'I'm not surprised you want to keep him, Sarah. He's

59

adorable. But he'll be better off with the vet. How could anyone kill something like that?'

'That's what we've still got to find out,' Kit said grimly, standing up. 'We've got to find out who shot his mum! I'm going out to see if Dan's found any more clues.'

10

What next for Button?

Sarah looked up at the clock, and sighed. Would the vet never come? Jenny saw her look, and reached out to put her arm across Sarah's shoulder. Both girls were sitting on the floor, near the box where Button was still fast asleep.

'I'm sure he won't be much longer. I wonder when the boys will get back. It's awful just waiting for things isn't it?'

'Let's talk about something else,' Sarah suggested. 'Something to take our minds off the waiting.'

'Will Kit still be here for Easter Sunday?' Jenny asked.

'No, his parents are picking him up on Saturday. Why?'

'Well, we're going to have a really good service. Dad's planning lots of exciting things to happen, and I know we're going to have some really good songs. It's a shame Kit will miss it, now he's a Christian too, because I don't expect his parents would take him, would they?'

'I don't think he'd understand it, even if they did,' Sarah laughed. 'They're taking him to Israel for a week after they pick him up.'

'Wow! Lucky Kit!' Jenny thought how lovely it would be to go to Israel and see all the places they read about in the Bible.

'Do you think he'll send us postcards?' she asked rather wistfully.

At that moment the back door opened and Kit and Daniel came in.

'Postcards from where?' Daniel demanded.

'From Israel, when Kit goes!'

'Of course I will. I'll take lots of photos too. Wouldn't it be good if you could all come too, like you did last summer.'

'We're all going on the church holiday. It's a shame you can't come to that!'

'Maybe next year!' Kit said. He'd asked his parents about the church holiday, but they hadn't wanted him to go. And Israel would be fun. It was just a shame he couldn't have both!

'Did you find any clues?' Jenny changed the subject.

'Yes, there are a lot more footprints, even since this morning, I think. The mud's quite trampled where we saw them before. But we can't work out why. We thought maybe we could all go and see tomorrow. Perhaps between the lot of us, we'll be able to work out what it's all about.'

'But we came back to find out what the vet said,' Kit chipped in.

'He hasn't been yet.' Sarah glanced down at Button. 'I do wish he'd hurry up!'

'I don't expect he'll be much longer,' Jenny said soothingly. 'It's over an hour now.'

And she was right. A few minutes later there was a ring at the door bell, and then Mrs Masters appeared with a tall man carrying a black case, like a doctor's.

'Sarah, this is Mr White, the vet,' Mrs Masters said. 'The fox cub is in that box there, Mr White. Come on, you three, we'll leave Sarah and Mr White to talk about him. It's too crowded with all of us in this tiny kitchen.'

Jenny scrambled to her feet, and she and Daniel headed for the door. Sarah threw Kit a pleading look. She hated being alone with strangers.

'Would it be all right, if I stayed too, sir? You see, I was with Sarah just after she found Button.' Kit's polite 'talking to adults' tone had the desired effect on Mr White, who smiled and nodded, but it sent Daniel and Jenny upstairs in fits of giggles.

'Do you remember how he used to talk like that all the time? Super polite and grown-up?' Daniel said.

'Yes, he's certainly changed since we first met him,' Jenny said. 'For the better I think. He was a bit too grown-up sometimes.'

'Still, it's jolly useful, being able to turn it on like that. He's a good PR man,' Daniel said.

'A what?'

'Public Relations! You know, talking to strangers, keeping the grown-ups happy!'

Back in the kitchen Mr White had just heard how Sarah had found Button and how they'd tried to look after him.

'But he isn't well, and he isn't eating his food. He isn't going to die too, is he?' Sarah finished, plaintively.

'Well, now, I don't think so. But you did the right thing, getting your mum to call me. It isn't easy to look after a fox, anyway, and this one is very young. People think you can treat them just like dogs, but that's not true; they're wild animals and need to be treated accordingly. Now, young lady, lift him out, and I'll examine him.'

Sarah carefully lifted the sleepy fox cub out of the box. He yawned, and his little pink tongue flicked out. Then he opened his eyes and whined.

'Lay that woolly thing on the table and put him there,' the vet said. Sarah put Button down and as usual, he grabbed the jumper in his teeth, and turned round with it.

'There's still some play in him, anyway,' Mr White

commented. 'Good! Now young fellow, let's have a look at you.'

He reached out towards the fox.

'Oh, be careful, he bit Mum!' Sarah warned.

Mr White smiled. 'I don't think he'll bite me.'

He didn't! Mr White held him gently but firmly, and examined his teeth, felt his nose, ran a hand over his body, and looked at his ears.

'I don't think there's a lot wrong with him,' he said at last. 'He's about five weeks old, I would say, and a bit small for his age so probably what you've been feeding him hasn't been quite what he needed.'

'He didn't seem to want to eat much, sir!' Kit explained. 'We gave him milk, and sometimes he would drink it. We tried him with puppy food, and some cooked liver. Mostly he just left it.'

'I think the milk was too rich for him,' the vet explained. 'Normally he would still be getting some milk from his mother, and that's quite different from cow's milk you know. Even human babies can't take cow's milk when they're very small. It upsets their tummies. Baby animals are the same; their own mother's milk is best. The puppy food should have suited him, that was good thinking. What made you get that?'

'I went to the library and read a book about foxes,' Kit explained. 'They seemed quite like dogs to me. We've got a friend who has a collie, and last year when he was small he had puppy food.'

'So we didn't feed him all the wrong things?' Sarah had been listening with a sinking feeling that they'd been slowly poisoning Button instead of looking after him.

'Oh no,' Mr White assured her. 'Probably he just needed feeding more frequently than you were able to do. Then he ate too much at once when he had the chance. I think he got a bit cold too. You kept him outside, didn't you?'

Sarah nodded.

'Normally at his age,' Mr White continued, 'he'd still be down in a nice warm den with all his brothers and sisters. Sometimes as many as six. All together underground they'd be snug and warm. He'd come out to play but still go underground to sleep and warm up. Your little fox has a chill, but we can soon sort that out.'

'What will you do with him?' Sarah asked. 'He'll be all right, won't he?'

'He'll be fine. I'm sure you saved his life, because left on his own in the wood he wouldn't have survived; he was too young to fend for himself. I'll take him back to the surgery now, and give him some antibiotics, and a nice warm cage. The nurses there will keep an eye on him overnight, and he'll soon be good as new.'

'Can I have him back then?'

Mr White frowned. 'You know, I don't really think that's a good idea. Foxes aren't like dogs; they can never be really house trained. They're destructive. They scratch the wallpaper off, bite and claw at the furniture, and attack strangers, especially if they are frightened. They are a real handful. They don't make good pets. Would your mother agree to a pet like that?'

Sarah sighed. She did so want to keep Button. Kit grinned.

'I can just imagine what mine would say!'

'But I don't want to lose him!' Sarah wailed. 'He's mine!'

'I'll see what I can think of,' Mr White promised. 'I'll have a chat with your mother on the way out. Now I'll just give him an injection to send him to sleep, so that he doesn't panic in the car, then you pop him back in his box and I'll take him off to the surgery. You can ring up tomorrow morning to find out how he's getting on, if you like.'

And with that Sarah had to be content.

11

Treasure hunt

Next morning when Sarah woke up, she couldn't think at first why she felt so miserable. As she gradually drifted up out of sleep, she remembered. Button had gone! I wish he'd stayed here, she thought. Then she remembered how weak and ill he had looked. If I'd kept him, he might have died. I love him so much, but I can't look after him properly, so he's got to go away. Why isn't loving enough?

Just then, there was a knock at her bedroom door, and Kit came in. He perched on the end of her bed and tucked his feet under the duvet.

'How do you feel today?' he asked.

'I want Button back,' Sarah told him. He opened his mouth to speak but she rushed on.

'I know, don't tell me! It's better for him if he's at the vet's. That doesn't stop me missing him.'

'I bet he's missing you too!'

'Do you really think he is?'

'I'm sure he is. Love works two ways, doesn't it? I know I miss you lot dreadfully when I first go back to school. And sometimes I miss my parents so much I could cry – except of course that you don't at school, at least not when anyone can find out, or you get teased something awful.'

'Poor Kit. I'd hate boarding school.'

'Oh, it's not that bad. It's only the first couple of days,

then you get used to it again. Anyway, I've got friends there now too. Most of the time it's good fun.'

They sat there in friendly silence for a few minutes. Sarah was thinking about Button missing her. I hope he begins to enjoy it soon too, like Kit does at school, she thought.

Kit was thinking about going back to school in a few weeks, beginning a new term, trying for the under eleven cricket team, swimming in the school pool. He was surprised to realise that he was almost looking forward to going back! Maybe it's not so bad being left in England; I know it's for my own good really. Before, I didn't understand how it could be, but now I'm beginning to see, he thought.

Suddenly Sarah threw her pillow at him.

'Come on, let's go and see if Dan's awake. We've got to solve the mystery of the footprints today.' And she scrambled out of bed, determined not to be miserable.

After breakfast, Mum dialled the vet's surgery and the vet came to speak to Sarah.

'Button had a good night. He's eaten well, and slept a lot. I think he's soon going to be all right. We'll keep him here for a few days, just to make sure. I've had an idea where the best place for him is, but I'd like to take you to visit it, as he's your fox, to see if you agree. It won't be today, but I might be able to fit it in tomorrow. Ask your mother to come back on the phone so I can make the arrangements, will you?'

Sarah put the receiver down beside the phone and went to get her mother. Then she ran out to the den where Kit and Daniel were waiting for the others. Jenny came through the garden gate when she was half way down the garden, so she waited for her.

'How's Kate?' Sarah asked.

'Not bad. She's only got it very mildly, so Mum thinks she will be able to come on the church holiday with us, if she just stays quiet for the first couple of days.'

'Oh good!' Kate was Sarah's best friend, and the only one of the gang who was the same age as her, so she was glad she would be able to come.

'She's sorry she missed seeing your fox,' Jenny continued, 'but she's had a good idea about the footprints and the dead foxes. She thinks they're linked together.'

'So does Daniel!'

By now they had come to the hedge, so they pushed their way through. On the other side, Kit, Daniel and James were waiting. Sarah turned to Daniel.

'Kate thinks the dead foxes and the footprints are linked, just like you do.'

'Does she?' Daniel had almost given up that idea because he'd racked his brains all night and still couldn't come up with the connection. 'How?' he asked Jenny.

'She's sent a note.' Jenny fished in her pocket and unfolded a piece of paper. They all pored over the coded message.

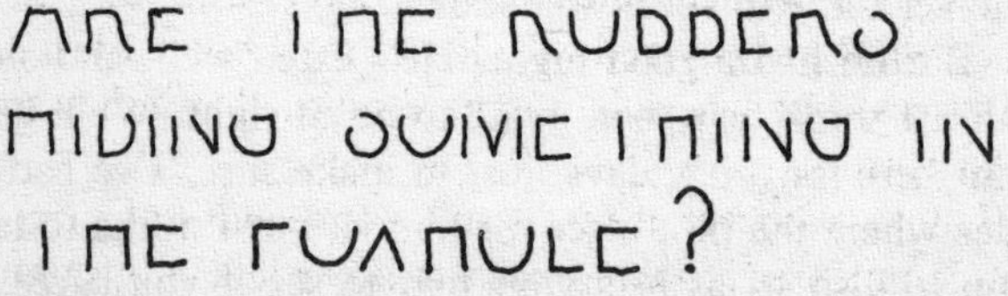

ᐱᑎᴇ ᴉ �∩ᴇ ᴎ∪ᗡᗡᴇᴎᴕ
ᴎIᗡIᴎᴕ ᴕᴑᴉᴎᴇ ᴉ ᴎIᴎᴕ IIᴎ
ᴉ ∩ᴇ ᴦ∪ᴧ∩∪ᴧᴇ ?

'Hiding something in the earth! Why ever didn't I think of that?'

'So there might be an earth somewhere near where all those footprints are. Let's go and see!' James was already halfway back through the bushes that hid the den from the rest of the wood.

'Hang on a minute!' Jenny pulled him back. 'If they are robbers, and they are hiding the stolen goods in the wood, we don't want to go rushing out there and bump into them. They might be violent.'

'So we post lookouts,' Daniel said. 'James, you and I

can do the searching. We're biggest, so it ought to be us. Sarah, Jenny and Kit can spread out on the paths leading to where the footprints are, and if anyone comes do the owl call, as loud as you can. Agreed?'

They all nodded.

'Right, let's go!'

One by one they pushed through the bushes and set off into the wood.

It was damp in the wood. It had rained for most of the night, and the leaves on the ground were still shiny with rainwater. The trees had raindrops hanging from the tips of the bare branches, and the trunks were dark from being soaked. But the rain had stopped now and there was a fresh earthy smell rising from the damp vegetation. Jenny sniffed appreciatively.

'I do love the country smell after rain!'

James laughed. 'It's been raining non-stop for a fort-night! You've been tucked up in bed away from it, but the rest of us are sick of the smell of wet greenery!'

The gang walked quietly on the damp ground. Where the ground was covered with leaves their booted feet left no traces, but where it was bare mud, they left a trail of footprints.

'I hope whoever it is doesn't notice our footprints,' Kit commented, looking back at a particuclarly muddy part of the path, marked now by five pairs of assorted wellies!

Soon afterwards, the path divided, and Daniel and James went off to the left, where the bank and the footprints were. Kit volunteered to stay at the place where the paths met to relay any signals if the girls were too far away to be heard. Sarah and Jenny went further into the wood. Near where the next join in the path was, there was a little group of hazel trees, with catkins beginning to come out.

'Let's stop here, and pick a couple of hazel branches,'

Jenny suggested. 'Then if anyone comes, we'll just look as if we're collecting them.'

'Good idea!' Sarah reached up and pulled off a branch. 'We'll give them to your mum to put in the church for Easter Day. That way they won't be wasted.'

James and Daniel made their way along the path that led to the steep bank.

'I think there are more footprints again today, don't you, James?'

'I'm not sure. They're all getting trodden in together. It's certainly a very well used path.'

'Strange, since it doesn't go anywhere!'

'Except to some buried treasure!'

Daniel shuddered. Suddenly, what they were doing seemed serious, and maybe a little dangerous.

'We didn't tell anyone where we were going. Do you think it's safe?' he asked James.

'I don't think robbers would bring their booty to hide in the middle of the day, do you?' James answered. 'They probably come at night. Anyway, we've got our spies out. They can't prove we know anything if we're just acting like kids playing in the wood.'

'No. . .' Daniel felt a bit worried about leaving the girls to keep watch like that. What if the men did come and were nasty to them. . .

'Come on, James, let's get it over with quickly.'

They began to run; slowly, because the path was very muddy and their boots slowed them down. When they reached the bank, they stopped, staring at it. The footprints disappeared into the drifted leaves, so there was no clue there. Most of the bank was covered with brambles and dead bracken.

'We've got to be careful not to disturb it. They mustn't know we've been here,' Daniel said.

'Foxes often dig out under tree roots. Let's start by looking there.' James clambered up towards the roots of a big oak tree, sticking out from the bank.

'Nothing here!' He slid down and moved along to the next one. Daniel copied, going the other way, pulling brambles aside, feeling into every nook and cranny. Gradually the two boys got further away from each other. Daniel had come round to thinking that their theory about the foxes' earth was wrong and was just about to suggest they give up and go home, when James called him.

'Dan, come here, quick! I've found something!'

12

Treasure found

Daniel scrambled down the muddy bank as fast as he could, and tore across to where James was standing, with his two hands thrust under a tangle of wet greenery and tree roots.

'What is it?' he whispered.

'Feels like a sack! It's got hard lumpy things inside. Hang on! I'll try and pull it out.'

'No, don't! If we disturb it, and the thieves come back, they'll know someone's been here and moved it. Are you sure there's something in there?'

'Positive! I'll come down and you can have a feel.'

So James jumped down and Daniel clambered up to where James had been standing. It was damp and muddy under the roots, but sure enough, as he pushed his hand into the hole, it came up against the rough cloth texture of a piece of sacking. Inside, he could feel things with hard sides, sharp corners and some smooth rounded things.

'Wow!' he breathed. 'We've done it! We've found the loot!'

He slid back down to join James.

'It's a fantastic hiding place,' James said. 'Look, even after we've been fiddling around, you can't tell there's anything there. Must have been a really good hiding place for a fox.'

'Not bad for hidden treasure, either,' Daniel giggled

nervously. Neither boy could really believe what was happening. They stood and stared at the tangle of greenery hiding the hole. Suddenly James gave a shudder and clutched Daniel's arm.

'Come on, let's get out of here! We're standing here like a couple of lemons and every minute we waste means there's more chance of the thieves coming back, and us getting caught.'

They turned and ran back along the muddy path, their footprints mingling with those that they now knew belonged to the robbers. Where the paths joined Kit was waiting. They stopped and all three together gave the owl call. Soon, Sarah and Jenny appeared round the bend, looking worried.

'Are you all right?' Jenny asked anxiously.

James and Daniel both nodded.

'We didn't know if the call meant you'd been seen,' Jenny said. 'What's happened?'

So, interrupting each other, with the words tumbling out, James and Daniel recounted what they had found.

'We've got to tell the police!' Jenny said.

'They won't believe us!' Sarah objected.

'Well, let's catch the robbers ourselves!' James was feeling braver now they were all together. 'We could set a booby trap for them!'

'Don't be so stupid, James Taylor,' Jenny said angrily. 'They could be really dangerous. After all we've been told about not talking to strangers, you want to go off and tackle two that we know are vicious.'

'We don't know for sure that they are the same two,' Daniel objected.

'Or even that there are only two. There might be lots more,' Kit said reasonably.

'All the more reason for not trying to tackle them ourselves,' Jenny stated firmly. 'We'll go to my dad and tell him. He'll convince the police that we're telling the truth.'

Sarah let out a sigh of relief. It was useful having a friend whose dad was the vicar; everyone had to believe what the vicar said!

As fast as they could they all raced round to the vicarage. Mr Williams was in his study writing, but when the childen burst in with their news, he put down his pen and listened. Then he phoned the police, and the gang listened anxiously to his end of the conversation. At last he put the phone down and turned back to the gang.

'There's a car coming round with some policemen in it,' he said. 'They want one of you to show them where you found the stolen goods, and then they want all of you to keep well away from the wood until the thieves have been caught.'

Daniel and James showed their disappointment on their faces. They had hoped to be there to see the men being arrested. But Mr Williams continued. 'I know you'd like to be there, but for your own safety you must stay well away. We'll let you know the outcome as soon as we can. Do I have your promise?'

The gang looked at each other. They knew they didn't really have any choice, so Daniel answered for all of them 'Yes, we promise to stay away.'

'Now who's going to show the police where to go?'

Daniel desperately wanted to, but before he could say so, Jenny said, 'James found it. He should go!'

Daniel sighed. That was only fair.

'Yes. James, you go.'

It wasn't long till the police car arrived, and James went off to show the men where the 'treasure' was. Jenny popped upstairs to tell her sister Kate the good news, but came down again straight away. Kate was asleep!

They trailed slowly back to Daniel and Sarah's house and gathered in Kit's bedroom, waiting for James to come back. In a few minutes he joined them.

'We're banished from the wood until further notice!' he announced. 'The wood's full of policemen hidden, waiting to catch the robbers when they come back to hide some more loot or collect what's already there. They said to make sure we stayed away.'

'There's ingratitude for you!' Daniel complained. '*We* found out what was going on, *we* found the loot, but we're not allowed to be there to see the baddies caught. It's not fair!'

'I agree!' James said. 'We should be in on the act!'

Jenny shuddered. 'No, thank you. I'm quite happy to let the police do the catching!'

'So am I!' Kit backed her up. 'Won't I have something to tell them all at school! They'll never believe me!'

'Neither will Robert, when he gets back.'

'And poor Kate. She's missed it all.' Sarah felt sorry for her special friend.

'It was her idea that made us look again, though,' Daniel reminded her. 'She was really as much part of it as the rest of us.'

'I think I'll go home now and see if she's woken up. I can't wait to tell her the news,' Jenny said. 'See you in church tomorrow.'

'Church?' Kit was puzzled. 'It's Friday tomorrow!'

'Good Friday. Church in the morning and hot cross buns for tea.' Jenny poked her head back round the door to remind him.

'I've never been to church on Good Friday before,' Kit said. 'Is it fun?'

'Well, no, it's quite a serious service. It's when we think about Jesus dying and what he left behind, and remember that he did it all for us,' James explained.

'But it's short! That's the best bit!' Daniel grinned.

Tomorrow! That's when I go to see Button's new home, between church and tea. I hope it's nice, Sarah thought. I wonder how he's getting on without me!

13

New home for Button?

Sarah was sitting in the passenger seat of the vet's car, watching the countryside streaming past as they drove along the winding country roads. After church Dad had taken her to the vet's surgery, where she'd spent a little while playing with Button. He looked a lot better, and had yapped his pleasure at seeing her. True to form, after a few minutes hectic chasing and pouncing, he'd grabbed Sarah's jumper, that she'd wrapped him in when she'd first found him, retreated back into his cage, pulling it with him, curled up in it and gone to sleep. Sarah was glad to see that he seemed to like his cage, though a little disappointed too, that he could be happy without her.

'He's doing fine,' Mr White, the vet, told her, as they got into his car. 'He's eating well, and putting on weight, and the nurses play with him. But he really needs to be with other foxes; young ones like him, and older ones too. I've found a place where they look after foxes until they can be released back into the wild. Some never can, and they keep those and look after them. They have several in a large enclosed wood. I think your Button will like it there.'

'Will Button be able to go out into the wild?' Sarah asked.

'I'm not sure. Sometimes foxes that have been hand reared lose their fear of humans so much that they just wouldn't be safe in the wild. They'd be killed by fox hunters or farmers because they wouldn't have the sense to run away. Others can't learn how to catch their own food so they need looking after too. But the people at this place are very good. They never let a fox go free unless they are sure it has a good chance of survival. Because you had him so young, and now he's been in the surgery, surrounded by people, I rather imagine Button will stay a semi-tame fox.'

'Does that mean I'll be able to visit him?'

'I don't know. We'll have to ask the people who run the centre.'

The conversation had fizzled out there, and now Sarah was watching the countryside flash by. She was beginning to come to terms with the idea of not having Button back, but she did hope she would be able to visit from time to time.

'Please, Lord Jesus,' she whispered, and suddenly something that Mr Williams had said in church that morning popped back into her head. He'd said; 'Sometimes love hurts.' Then he'd explained it by saying that God the Father loved Jesus, so he couldn't have wanted Jesus to die in that dreadful way, but he loved us too, so much that he allowed Jesus to be killed, because that was what was best for us. God's love for the world meant something happened to Jesus that seemed absolutely dreadful, but in the end it was the best thing.

How strange, Sarah thought now, that's just what Kit said. He'd thought at first that it was because his parents didn't love him enough that they left him behind at boarding school, but really it was because they did love him. Now that he's enjoying it, he must be able to see that it was the best thing really. I really do want the best thing for Button too, because I love him. And if that makes me miserable I'll just try to remember that God was hurt too when Jesus had to die to rescue us from all the wrong things we'd done.

Lost in her thoughts like this, Sarah hardly noticed the miles passing. It was strange, but she'd never really thought about God being hurt before. 'Sacrificial love' that was the long word Mr Williams had used. 'If you love someone enough you'll do whatever is best for them, no matter how much it hurts you; that's what Jesus did when he died.' And that's what I'll do for Button she decided. If it's best for him to go to this place I'll try not to mind. And with this settled in her head, she turned her attention back to the passing countryside.

Mr White saw her move in her seat.

'Nearly there!' he said. 'Just around the next bend there's a big white gate on the left. Look out for it.'

'There it is!' Sarah exclaimed, as the car came round the bend, and Mr White pulled into a gravel driveway that twisted away between two lines of trees.

At the end of the drive was a long low whitewashed house, with a twist of smoke rising lazily from the chimney. Behind on a slope was a small wood. As they got out of the car, a lady appeared from the front door. She was wearing jeans and a thick brightly patterned jumper, nd she had a lovely warm smile. Sarah liked her at once.

'Hello, you must be Sarah! I'm Donna MacWilson, but everyone around here calls me Mrs Fox. I hear you've got a baby fox who would like to come and live here, at White Cottage Farm, with us.'

'Sarah just wants to see for herself and make sure this is the right home for Button,' Mr White explained.

'Quite right too. If you've saved him and kept him alive, you want to be sure he's in good hands, don't you? Come on then, I'll show you around. David, there'll be a cup of coffee going in the office, if you ask Jane.'

Mr White, who was obviously David, smiled, said, 'See you later, Sarah,' and headed towards the front door.

Mrs Fox smiled at Sarah.

'Come round the back and I'll show you the pens where we keep the injured foxes.'

There followed one of the most interesting afternoons Sarah had ever spent in her life. For once, she didn't feel ill at ease and awkward with a stranger. Mrs Fox seemed to expect her to have the same love of, and interest in foxes as she did herself, and she obviously cared so much about the animals that Sarah soon found herself chatting away as if to an old friend.

The pens were half covered over, and in each one was a fox with some sort of injury. There was one with its leg in plaster, and another with a big bandage round its face and a funny collar like a lampshade round its neck. Mrs Fox explained that it was to stop the fox scratching at the bandage with its claws and so give the eye a chance to heal. Two of the pens had foxes curled up in them, seemingly asleep.

Further on, Mrs Fox showed her a large grassy enclosure where several fox cubs, slightly bigger than Button, were rolling around in a play battle, quite uncaring that there were people watching them.

'Button plays like that!' Sarah burst out, seeing one grab at a piece of grass and worry it, 'but he uses my shoe-lace!'

'It's the way they all play. Aren't they having fun together!'

Sarah realised that if she kept Button, he would never have the fun of playing with other cubs. These were obviously older than Button, their faces had the pointed look that adult foxes have, not the rather catty shape that Button still had, and their fur was more gingery than his.

'How old are these?' she asked.

'About ten weeks. They came in a sack. Someone had found them all together. He thought they had been abandoned. I think the mother was probably just moving them from one earth to another, and had gone back for another one, but anyway, once they'd come here, there was no point trying to get them back to the mother, so we just had to keep them.'

'Does that happen often?'

'Yes, very often people see a lone fox cub and think it's been abandoned, whereas the mother is really quite close by. Look, over here is the wood, where the foxes live which we hope to reintroduce to the wild. There are about seven in there at the moment. You won't see them because they'll be lying up somewhere sheltered. We leave them alone as much as possible, so they'll learn how to cope in the wild.'

Sarah peered into the wood, but couldn't see any foxes.

'What about the ones you keep?' she asked, 'the ones that can't go back?'

'They are round the other side in another large wooded area. Come on, this way.'

As they came around the other side of the house, Mrs Fox started making the sort of noise people usually use to call a dog, and behind the fence, as if from nowhere, two foxes appeared wagging their tails and yapping.

'Button does that!' Sarah exclaimed delightedly.

'That's their "Pleased to see you" noise.' Mrs Fox leaned over the fence and rubbed one fox's ears. It made a low rumbling noise almost like a purr.

'This one's Beaut. He's just a year old. He was brought to us when he was two weeks old, and he's lived here ever since. That one over there is Lady. She's shy of strangers. There are also a couple of four month old cubs in there that'll stay with us. We've also got a little one like your Button indoors, who needs feeding up as he's been very ill, who'll come out here when he's better. This is where Button would live, and you could come and see him whenever you wanted.'

'Really?'

'Yes, you'll always be special to him, because you fed him when he was little. Come as often as you can. He'll still be your fox.'

Sarah sighed. She knew Button would be happier here than at home shut in somewhere on his own.

'Will he come to us?' Mrs Fox asked. 'We'd love to have him.'

Sarah took a big breath. She had to make the decision and stick by it. Inside she knew that it was really already made. This place seemed ideal for him.

'Yes, please!' she said.

14

The mystery solved

Back in the car, clutching the postcard showing fox cubs playing happily together that Mrs Fox had given her as she left, Sarah felt rather mixed up. Strangely, the top feeling was one of relief; now she wouldn't have to be responsible for Button. Someone else, who knew much better how to do it, would look after him. There was also sadness, because she had wanted to keep him for her very own pet, but after all, she could still visit as often as someone could be persuaded to drive her over, and there was always Dennis, James' dog, at home. He was almost part of the gang, and had probably felt very left out of their adventures over the last few days. Having been brought up on a farm, he would have found it very hard to make friends with a fox! Then there was her love for Button; she would always love him, but now she could see that loving him had to mean letting him go, even if that hurt. She sighed.

'Sad?' Mr White asked, quietly.

Sarah considered.

'No, not really. I would have liked to keep him, but this is better for him, isn't it? It's a lovely place and Mrs Fox is really nice. She'll look after him better than I could.'

'That's right. He's really a wild animal, not a house pet. Here he can be free and happy, and that should make you happy too.'

Sarah remembered the fox cubs she'd seen tumbling over each other. Yes, Button would enjoy that. And I'm going on holiday next week, she thought happily. He'll be settled by then. What would I have done with him at home?

The journey back didn't seem nearly as far, and it wasn't long before Sarah was jumping out of the car, outside her garden gate. Stuck on the front of it was a message in code. Sarah waved goodbye to Mr White and then took down the message.

SARAH
COME TO DEN AT ONCE
GOOD NEWS.

Sarah raced down the garden to the den, pausing just to yell 'Mum, I'm back!' through the open kitchen door. Scrambling through the hedge, to where the other members of the gang were waiting for her, she collapsed in a panting heap.

'What's the news?' she gasped.

'They've caught the thieves!' Daniel announced importantly.

'What!' Sarah shouted. 'How? When? Tell me!'

'Last night. . . .'

'They set a guard round the. . . .'

'There was another robbery. . . .'

'It was who. . . .'

Four voices started at once, then collapsed into giggles.

'Come on!' Sarah urged, impatiently. 'Jenny, you tell me!'

'Well, you know the police set up a watch all round the foxhole. Nothing happened until late last night. Then they saw two men coming into the wood with a bin liner with things in it.'

'They'd done another robbery,' James interrupted.

'Over towards school.'

'And they were bringing the loot to hide,' Jenny carried on. 'The police let them get to the hole, then caught them.'

'The policeman came to tell us, this afternoon, while you were out.' Daniel took up the story. 'He said we'd been very clever to track them down like that.'

'And he thinks it probably was those two men who were nasty to James and me,' Kit added, with satisfaction. 'They'd decided to use the foxes' earth to hide the loot in. They'd done it once before apparently and got away with it. So they watched out for the vixen, and tracked her back to her hole. Then they shot her, and two of her cubs, but two others escaped.'

'That must have been Button and the one James' dad found,' Sarah said. 'What happened to the other two? Why didn't Mr Taylor find the bodies?'

'They buried them under some dead leaves. Anyway, once the earth was empty, they started stealing things and hiding them. I'm glad they got caught!' Kit ended.

James filled in the rest of the story. 'The policeman said they'll be charged with cruelty to animals as well as theft.'

'And we helped to catch them. Wow!' Sarah's satisfied comment went for all of them.

The gang felt thoroughly proud of themselves. They sat there for a few moments, smugly, then Kit asked, 'What happened about Button?'

So Sarah told them about Mrs Fox and White Cottage Farm.

'The vet's going to take him over tomorrow to settle him in,' she finished. 'He said I could go too, but I don't know if I want to.'

'Anyway, don't forget I'm leaving tomorrow, too,' Kit

reminded her.

'And Mum said we've got to sort out our clothes for the church holiday,' Daniel added. 'There'll be plenty to do here.'

'But wouldn't you like to see him settled in, and know he's happy?' Jenny asked.

'Mmm, maybe. Anyway, the vet's going to ring and find out if I'm going, so I don't have to decide yet.'

'I'm glad that's turned out well, too,' Kit said. 'I couldn't have stood it if I'd had to go away, not knowing how things turned out for Button.'

Sarah had an idea.

'Why don't you come too? To settle him in, I mean. I'm sure we could fit it in before your parents take you away.'

'That'd be great!' Kit considered. 'They're not coming till after lunch. When is your vet going to take Button?'

'After morning surgery. I'm sure he wouldn't mind if you came too.'

'I'd like that.'

'Let's go in and ask Mum.'

'I'd better go, too,' James said. 'It's nearly milking time.'

So Sarah and Kit crawled through the hedge and up to the house, while James pushed his way through the rhododendron bushes and disappeared into the wood.

Left behind, Daniel grinned ruefully.

'Before Kit, it would have been me going too!'

'Poor Dan!' Jenny sympathised. 'Do you really mind?'

'A bit!' Daniel admitted. 'Sarah and Kit have had a great time with Button while I was ill. Still, I suppose it's only fair that he goes with her. He did help her look after him.'

Jenny thought she knew how Daniel felt. It was hard to be left out.

'Kit doesn't get much family life,' she said gently.

'You get to do things with Sarah and the rest of us, all through term time. He only has a couple of weeks a year.'

'I know, but that doesn't stop it hurting. Sarah and I have always done things together.'

'Never mind. Come and see Kate with me, and tell her the news. You'll be all right because you've had the pox. She doesn't know yet that her idea led to the thieves being caught.'

'No . . . poor Kate. She's more left out than me! I'll stop feeling sorry for myself.' Daniel stood up and grinned at Jenny. It was good to have a friend who sympathised and understood like Jenny did. He held out his hand to pull her up too.

'Come on, let's go and cheer Kate up!'

15

Button settles in

Mr Masters dropped Sarah and Kit off at the vet's surgery early the next morning. It had been agreed that both of them could go to settle Button into his new home, and the vet had suggested that they might like to spend some time with Button before he went. Sarah jumped at the chance, partly because she wanted to see Button again but also because she had decided that she wanted to be a vet, or someone who rescued animals, like Mrs Fox, when she grew up. She wanted to see all she could of what happened at a vet's.

When they arrived they were taken through to the back where the cages for sick animals were. Button was very much livelier than he had been even the last time Sarah had seen him. He gave a delighted yap of pleasure when he saw then, and started jumping up at the bars of his cage.

'He does behave just like a puppy!' Kit exclaimed. 'But he's beginning to look more like a fox. Look at his ears!'

Sarah looked. It was true. Button's nose looked more pointed than it had when she'd first found him, and his ears were more pointed than they had been.

'His fur's lighter and smoother than it used to be too,' she commented, dropping to her knees in front of the cage and stroking him through the bars.

One of the veterinary nurses lifted Button out, and

showed Sarah and Kit into a little room. She put Button down on the floor. He immediately pounced at Sarah's shoes.

'I'll leave you two here to play with him,' the nurse said. 'He's quite better now, and back up to the weight he should be. Don't open the door, will you! We don't want him to escape. But if you can tire him out, it'll make the journey easier for all of you.'

And she closed the door behind her.

Sarah sat on the floor and hugged Button tight. Tearfully she looked up at Kit.

'I'm going to miss him so much!'

Kit looked down at his friend. He knew it was hurting her. But he also thought he knew what might help.

'That's how I felt when I said goodbye to my parents at school. It feels as if it'll never get better. But it does, you know. Gradually it doesn't hurt so much and at last you find you're actually enjoying things again. It'll be like that for you too.'

He hesitated, then plunged on 'And of course, there's always Jesus. Last term, coming up to Christmas, when I had that awful lonely time, you know, when I wrote you that awful sorry-for-myself letter, I felt as if no one had ever felt like that before. Then I read in the Bible where it says Jesus gave up being with God, so he could do what God wanted and die on the cross, and I realised that he must have been lonelier than anyone ever before or after has been. He'd left heaven, and God his Father, and come to men to be their friend and to die for them, and they didn't even want him. That made me realise he understands how I felt. He knows how you feel too.'

He fell silent, embarrassed. It was strange how hard it was to talk about that time, even to Sarah, who was a friend and a Christian too. During those few awful lonely weeks, Kit had come to realise how much Jesus loved him and how good it was to have a friend who would always be there.

Sarah looked down at Button, then up at Kit and smiled a rather wobbly smile.

'It's strange, those things keep coming up this Easter. About how loving is wanting the best for the person you love, and doing what's best for them even if it hurts. Me and Button. Your parents leaving you at school. Jesus dying so we could be friends with God, 'cos that's the only way it could happen. Up until now, I always thought love was a happy feeling.'

'It is!' Kit assured her. 'Sometimes it feels sad, but the happiness is there underneath. I'm glad my parents love me even when they're hundreds of miles away.'

Just then Button got tired of being held so tightly, and nipped Sarah's hand. She put him down on the floor and they spent a riotous half hour chasing him around the room, throwing a little ball for him to catch, and playing tug of war with Kit's hankie.

All too soon, the door opened, and Mr White came in carrying a wire travel box in which was Sarah's jumper, by now hardly recognisable.

'Ready?' he asked.

Sarah nodded, suddenly too choked to speak.

'Good girl. Pop Button in here. I hope he'll settle down and sleep. Have you worn him out?'

'We've worn ourselves out!' Kit said as he stood up and shook the hair back from his eyes.

'Come on, Sarah. Let's go!'

Sarah lowered Button onto the jumper in the box, and Mr White fixed the lid. Then the three of them went out to his car. Sarah got into the back seat and Mr White put Button in his travel box on the seat beside her. Kit strapped himself into the front passenger seat. Mr White started the engine, and they were off.

Button didn't like it! He howled, he scratched at the wire of the box, he snarled, he growled. Kit put his hands over his ears. Sarah tried to stroke Button, but he wouldn't keep still. He threw himself from one side of the box to the other, and Sarah had to give all her attention to stopping him rocking the box off onto the floor of the car. She was trying hard not to cry, too, because he was so upset.

'Don't worry, Sarah,' Mr White reassured her. 'He'll soon go to sleep.'

It didn't seem likely, but sure enough in a little while he flopped down on the jumper, yawned and fell asleep, whimpering a little at first. When at last he was quiet, Sarah felt in her jeans pocket for her hankie, and hastily dried her eyes. She didn't want Mrs Fox or the vet to know she'd been crying.

The rest of the journey went quietly. Now that Sarah knew the way it didn't seem so far, and Button didn't wake again until Mr White turned the ignition off at White Cottage Farm. Mrs Fox was there to meet them. Mr White carried the box with Button in it indoors to a room with two huge cages in it. In one was one other little cub about the same size as Button. Mrs Fox lifted him out, held him towards Sarah to stroke then put him gently down inside the cage. Kit put his arm across Sarah's shoulder, just so she'd know she wasn't alone.

They all held their breath, watching Button and the other little fox. Would they fight? Button stood where he had been put for a few minutes, crouching as if frightened. The other fox cub came slowly towards him, whining slightly, then put out a paw and tapped Button's nose. Button yapped at him, and then suddenly the two of them were tumbling over each other play fighting. Soon they were racing around the cage playing with a bit of stick, snarling and pouncing at it and each other.

Sarah let her breath out.

'He's made friends!' Mrs Fox said. 'He'll be happy now, learning to be a fox like other foxes. Don't worry about him, Sarah!'

Soon it was very difficult to work out which was Button; there was just a jumble of happy fox cubs having fun together.

Sarah bent down by the wire netting.

'Oh Button!' she whispered.

Immediately, one of the bundles of dark ginger fur extricated itself from the other and came trotting over to the fence. He nosed at Sarah's hand, and then trotted back to join his new friend. Sarah turned an ecstatic face up towards Mrs Fox.

'He heard me!' she breathed. 'He came to me!'

'He loves you!' Mrs Fox told her. 'He won't forget you if you come regularly to see him. Now let's leave him to get to know his new brother. I've got something for you in the kitchen.'

'Kit and I will join you in a minute,' Mr White said. 'I'd just like to show him the other pens.'

'Fine! Come on then, Sarah!'

The 'something' turned out to be a framed photograph of a tiny fox cub.

'This is the cub that is in with Button. That's what he looked like when we first had him,' Mrs Fox told her. 'I thought you'd like to have a picture of Button's new friend.'

'Thank you, it's lovely.' Sarah felt weepy again, as she realised she hadn't got a picture of Button.

That night, in bed, with Button gone, and Kit gone too, for a holiday with his parents, Sarah prayed, hugging the photograph to her, 'Lord Jesus, it hurts. Please help it to stop hurting soon. Please look after Button . . . and Kit.'

16

Medals for the gang

Easter Sunday morning dawned sunny for the first time in weeks. Sarah woke up feeling happy. She stretched, and snuggled back down into bed, trying to get back into the lovely dream she had been having about Button and his friend playing in the den. But as always happens when you really don't want to wake up, she found the dream slipping away from her and reality breaking in. The happy feeling faded as she remembered that Button had gone, and so had Kit, and even the thought of Easter eggs didn't really make up for the double loss. It was a tradition in the Masters family that breakfast on Easter Day didn't have to be good for you, and could consist of chocolate Easter eggs. Sarah dressed quickly and ran downstairs.

In the kitchen Daniel and Dad were already sitting at the table, and her mother was just putting mugs of coffee on the table. By each place there were two or three packages, which were obviously the cardboard containers for Easter eggs. Sarah had an extra package at her place; a flat square package, that couldn't possibly be an egg.

'Open that one first, Sarah!' Daniel urged her. 'I've never seen an egg that shape before.'

Sarah turned the flat parcel over. No clues outside as to what it was or who it was from. Puzzled, she began to unwrap it. Inside, to her delight, she found a photograph, just like the one Mrs Fox had given her.

'A photo of Button!' Sarah gasped. 'How wonderful!'
A slip of paper fell out too. Sarah put the photo carefully
down on the table and picked up the paper to read:

'Happy Easter Sarah,

Mr White and I thought you would like a photo of
Button. We took it yesterday while you were inside with
Mrs Fox and I was seeing round. I hope you like it.
Love Kit.'

'Wow! It's from Kit!' she announced after a little
while. 'Mr White planned it. He took the photo yesterday. So now I've got one of Button too.'

And abandoning her breakfast, she ran upstairs with
the photo, and placed it with the other one on her book-
case.

'There, now I've got you as well as your friend,
Button!' she said. 'Have a happy Easter, little one!'

From then on, the day seemed to get better. Sarah
enjoyed her breakfast; chocolate eggs made a lovely
change from boiled ones! Then they all went off together
to the happy Easter service. Sarah whispered to Jenny
about the photo, and Jenny gave her a hug to show she
was pleased.

Mr Williams talked about how after the pain and
loneliness of Good Friday, Easter came. When Jesus
came back to life, that brought joy to Jesus himself, to
God the Father and to people who trusted Jesus. Sarah
found herself bubbling over with joy too. She'd had to
let Button go, and that was sad, but he'd got new friends,
and so had she – Mrs Fox, and Mr White the vet. Button
had helped them to solve the mystery of the dead fox,
and the burglars had been caught, so the people would
all get their stolen things back.

It has all turned out right, she thought, as she stood
up to join in singing the last joyful hymn as loudly as
she could.

A fortnight later, Sarah was in her bedroom writing a letter to Kit, so that he'd have one waiting at school when he got back from Israel. It was taking a long time, because she was doing it in code, but she had a lot to tell him. There was the photo of Button to thank him for, there was all the news about the church holiday, but most important, she had to send his medal. The local policeman had given each member of the gang a little medal with a picture of a fox on it, as a way of saying well done for helping to catch the robbers.

Every so often, Sarah paused to suck her pencil, and looked at her two photos of the baby foxes. It turned out to be a good holiday after all, she thought, and went back to her letter. . . .

THE MEDAL WILL HELP
YOU REMEMBER ABOUT
THIS HOLIDAY. THANKS ·
FOR HELPING ME WITH
BUTTON. IF IT WASN'T
FOR HIM WE'D NEVER
HAVE STARTED LOOKING
FOR CLUES.
I THINK I LEARNED A
LOT ABOUT HOW
MUCH GOD LOVES US

YOU, THIS HOLIDAY,
SEE YOU AT HALF
TERM SARAH

At last she sighed and put down her pencil. 'There, that's done! I wonder what the next school holidays will bring. Not another fox in the den, that's for sure!'